WOMEN IN CRISIS:
STORIES FROM THE EDGE

Women in Crisis: Stories from the Edge

A collection of short stories
by

SUSAN L. POLLET

Adelaide Books
New York / Lisbon
2020

WOMEN IN CRISIS: STORIES FROM THE EDGE
A collection of short stories
By Susan L. Pollet

Copyright © by Susan L. Pollet
Cover design © 2020 Adelaide Books
Cover image: Susan L. Pollet

Published by Adelaide Books, New York / Lisbon
adelaidebooks.org
Editor-in-Chief
Stevan V. Nikolic

For any information, please address Adelaide Books
at info@adelaidebooks.org
or write to:
Adelaide Books
244 Fifth Ave. Suite D27
New York, NY, 10001

ISBN: 978-1-952570-64-3

Printed in the United States of America

Contents

Introduction   **9**

Prologue   **11**

Chapter One
Tokophobia: A Pathological Fear of Childbirth   **13**

Chapter Two
*Bipolar Disorder: An Adult Daughter's Struggle
with Her Mother's Illness and Death*   **20**

Chapter Three
Inheritance Stolen: the Pain of Being a Sibling   **33**

Chapter Four
Betrayal   **47**

Chapter Five
Parental Alienation   **64**

Chapter Six
Addiction **72**

Chapter Seven
Parental Kidnapping **82**

Chapter Eight
Child Abuse **92**

Chapter Nine
*Teen Dating Violence
and Revenge Pornography* **104**

Chapter Ten
Toxic Family **113**

Chapter Eleven
Body Image and Weight **124**

Chapter Twelve
Senior Seeking Peace: Elder Suicide **136**

Chapter Thirteen
Adoptee Seeking Closure **148**

Chapter Fourteen
Criminal Husband **161**

Chapter Fifteen
On-Campus Sexual Assault   **172**

Afterword   **183**

Acknowledgements   **185**

About the Author   **187**

Introduction

This book consists of stories about women patients of an accomplished woman psychiatrist, whose experiences exemplify challenges faced by many women, to varying degrees. I drew from my observations as a lawyer who worked on thousands of cases in Family Court for over twenty years, from my participation as a leader in women's bar associations for almost forty years, from listening to friends, colleagues and strangers, and from researching and reading the work of mental health professionals. The legal aspects of these stories are not the focus, but, rather, are a background component. It is the human aspects of the struggles of women in crisis which I found compelling, and it is for that reason that I chose the vehicle of a psychiatrist to bring them to the fore. In addition, I brought a feminist and humanist perspective to my presentation, as many of the conflicts women face are the result of a society which still makes them second class citizens.

Life stories are told to me spontaneously, and I seek them out. For whatever reason, and I have yet to fully understand it, people often tell me their deepest fears and concerns, whether they are close friends, or individuals whom I have met, for example, on public transportation and at other venues. It is not unusual for people to tell me that a confidence or secret they are telling me is being revealed for the first time. I hope that they see kindness in me and a safe harbor for their thoughts. Additionally, as the Archive and Historian for a women's bar association for approximately the last twenty years, I have interviewed hundreds of our members in order to publish their stories in a monthly newsletter to inspire the membership.

Thus, I have heard and collected many stories. I have absorbed the fears, secrets, and triumphs of those who have chosen to tell their stories to me. In this work, I have combined these stories as part of the creative process, changed names and details, and even imagined some of the stories based upon my reservoir of knowledge from years of being steeped in these issues. It is my hope that the reader, female or male, will have moments of recognition about themselves or people they know, that it will make them feel less alone, and that it will inspire them to make a positive difference in their own or someone else's life.

Prologue

My name is Esther Mahler. I am a board certified psychiatrist who has been practicing psychiatry, mostly in private practice, for over fifty years in New York City. I attended an Ivy League medical school when there were few women admitted, and when there were even fewer females who eventually specialized in psychiatry. It is no surprise that I had to be tougher, work harder, and sacrifice more of my personal life than others. At that time, there was no separate bathroom for women at the medical school. Women were made to feel unwelcome on a host of levels, including being told by the Dean that they were taking the place of a qualified man. Deep within me, I knew that I did belong and that I could make a contribution. I was able to listen to my own voice. I was strong enough for the struggle, in my case, because I had parents who encouraged me, so I had their voices supporting me as well.

As a result of these experiences, I eventually concentrated my private practice on helping women of all ages achieve their full potential. In all of the stories that I heard from my patients, their fears and hopes were inextricably linked with a society which disadvantages women on multiple levels. I had come to that conclusion many years before the feminist movement grew in the 1970's, and the current #MeToo Movement.

My family and friends sometimes called me "bossy." I like to think of that as a strength. I have never tried to impose my feminism on my patients, but my orientation toward making them strong, resilient and balanced is borne from that point of view. Their struggles have defined my life, much as I hope my treatment has improved theirs.

I have chosen to discuss certain patients, each at different stages of life, who embody issues many women face at differing levels of intensity. These stories are not grouped chronologically by their ages or by their diagnoses, because when I treated patients, they would come to me in no particular order, and we would sort through their issues together. The way I tell their stories reflects that randomness, and the pattern of their accounts.

Chapter One

Tokophobia:
A Pathological Fear of Childbirth

"Nothing in life is to be feared. It is only to be understood."

Marie Curie

One patient's difficulties comes to mind as illustrative of the conflicts of women throughout the ages, on a primal level. Anxieties related to childbirth are common in women. Despite advances in medicine, many women suffer from the fear of injury or death during delivery. This patient, whom I will refer to as Rhea, was thirty-eight years old at the time that I first treated her. She came into my office in an agitated state. She had been referred by her Obstetrician/Gynecologist for a consult. I eventually concluded that Rhea suffered from tokophobia, also known as maieusiophobia or parturiphobia, which is a pathological fear of childbirth. It was first described in the literature in 1897. Apparently, the prevalence of tokophobia in Western countries is over 20%. It had led Rhea to avoid pregnancy, although she desperately wanted to have a family. She was not only afraid of the pregnancy and birth experience, but she greatly feared that her child would be deformed.

On her first visit to my office, she sat down and immediately began to cry. She was an underweight, petite woman, who was well groomed and stylishly dressed in the manner of well-to-do Upper East Side women in Manhattan. She wore expensive jewelry and shoes, and carried a designer handbag. She appeared to be much younger than her years because of Botox injections and filler. I handed her tissues, and she slowly regained her composure. I asked her why she came to see me. She told me that she had been married for five years to a successful cardiologist, and that they lived a comfortable life in an expensive area of New York City's Upper East Side. They did not have a family support system as her family lived in California, and his family lived in Michigan. They had some friends, but she remained lonely much of the time.

She said that she quit working about six months prior for the express purpose of getting pregnant and starting a family. She had been a buyer for a major department store and the work involved a lot of travel and stress. She ceased having sex with her husband after she stopped birth control because she was afraid of pregnancy and childbirth. She was very trim and athletic. She ran ten miles and exercised two hours each day. She greatly feared what a pregnancy would do to her body. She said that her husband married her in large measure because of her beauty, and she was afraid he would not love her anymore if her body changed.

She believed that she would be unable to deliver a baby, and that if she would go into labor, she would die. She said she would not want to go into labor, and that she would never deliver vaginally, only by caesarean section, but she greatly feared that surgery as well. She felt tortured because she had an overwhelming desire to be a mother. She said that being a mother was more important to her than her career. Her husband was beginning to lose patience with her, and she feared that her marriage was in jeopardy as well. He wanted a large family, and she believed that another of the major reasons he had married her was because he thought she wanted that too.

I asked her when her fear of childbirth began. She related that her dread of childbirth began in adolescence after her maternal Uncle had sexually abused her while he was visiting her family home for the weekend one Christmas. He was a beloved Judge in a small town. He came to her bedroom in the middle of the night and tried to rape her, but she was able to escape. She never told anyone what had happened. It was too shameful for her, and her mother was close to him and probably would not have believed her, nor would anyone else because of his stature in the community.

Rhea said that after that, she had a series of monogamous relationships with different boyfriends until she met her now husband, and had engaged in sex with each boyfriend beginning at age eighteen. She was scrupulous in her use of contraceptives, and used several methods including the pill and IUD. She required her partners to use condoms at all times, in addition. She never had an accidental pregnancy. She continued to use the same contraceptive methods with her husband, but had stopped using contraception six months ago. That was when her depression and fears intensified, and she stopped having sex with him.

I asked her what her symptoms felt like. She replied to me in a monotonous tone.

"Since I stopped using contraception, Dr. Mahler, I have been having symptoms similar to what I had when my Uncle tried to rape me. That incident was so traumatic for me as I always thought he was a beloved Uncle when I was a child. I have shortness of breath, rapid breathing, my heartbeat becomes irregular, and I sweat and get nauseous. When it gets really bad, I start shaking, and I cannot even articulate a word or sentence. I guess it is like a panic attack. I also have suffered from depression for many years due to that trauma, but those feelings have intensified lately. I am sad, I feel guilty, I do not want to eat, I start crying uncontrollably, I cannot sleep well, and I feel helpless, hopeless and worthless much of the time. I have even considered suicide. Nobody in my family has a history of mental illness, so I feel very alone in my feelings. I do not want to burden my friends with these issues as they all have children and do not seem to share my issues."

I asked her if anything recently had triggered her feelings of panic and depression, other than the fact that she stopped using contraception. She replied:

"I turned thirty-eight-years-old six months ago. I became increasingly concerned that if I waited any longer, I would not be able to have any children. My husband has been putting pressure on me to get pregnant since we got married. When I consulted my Obstetrician/Gynecologist about getting pregnant, she ordered some tests, and told me that I was underweight and might have trouble getting pregnant unless I gained about ten pounds. I asked her about the complications of pregnancy. She told me about the pain of going into labor, and many complications, including changes to my body, the potential for a deformed fetus, eclampsia, premature delivery, infections, bleeding, embolism into the lungs, and even death of the baby or mother. After that discussion my fears intensified to a painful degree. It was at that point that I started to have less interaction with my husband on every level, and

I withdrew from my family and friends. I did not feel like spending time with anyone, and stayed in my apartment, alone and shaking much of the time."

I asked her if there was anything else that happened which triggered those feelings. She continued:

"Soon after I had the appointment with my Obstetrician/ Gynecologist, I met a friend for lunch from my prior job. She had just had her third baby, and was on maternity leave. She told me in great detail about her experiences of pregnancy and childbirth with each child and about her miscarriages. Her last birth experience was traumatic as the cord was wrapped around the baby's neck, and she had excessive bleeding after the birth. I started to get dizzy, and almost fainted as she was speaking. My mouth became dry, and I ran to the bathroom and sat on the toilet for about ten minutes with my head between my legs. The room was spinning."

I asked her why she thought she reacted that way.

"Dr. Mahler-I realized that I am in an impossible situation with no way out. My marriage depends on my being attractive and having children. I have terrible fears of losing control during my pregnancy and the delivery. I have fear of pain. I always had a fear of doctors, hospitals and needles. I have a fear of death from pregnancy. My maternal great grandmother died in childbirth as did three of her babies during prior deliveries. Even though there have been advances in medicine, my Obstetrician/Gynecologist told me that there is still a risk that these things could happen to me. If I don't have children, I will remain unhappy forever and I will lose my husband. And yet, if I become pregnant, I fear I will not be able to take it. There does not seem to be a solution."

I took Rhea on as a patient. I immediately started her on antidepressant medications. After about two weeks there was no improvement. I increased the dosages of the medications over the next month, and there was a reduction in her fear of pregnancy and her symptoms of depression. She began to have sex with her husband again. She did not suffer a recurrence of the symptoms while on the medications. She remained my patient for several years and came to me for weekly counseling sessions.

Ironically, it turned out that she was unable to get pregnant. She suffered from chronic anovulation, a common cause of infertility, due to her low body weight. In addition, her husband's sperm count was too low. She never gained the ten pounds she needed to in order to improve her chances of getting pregnant, and her husband would not give up his three glasses of wine per day and his saunas at the gym, which decreased his sperm count. Even in-vitro fertilization ('IVF') did not work. They ended up adopting two children, and she stayed home to raise them. At that point she stopped her counseling treatment with me and seemed to be coping well.

Lest you believe that Rhea's life remained uncomplicated since there seemed to be a satisfactory solution to Rhea's dilemma, when Rhea turned fifty, she returned to me for treatment for a short time. Her husband had left her for a much younger woman, he fought her over spousal and child support, and child custody, and she was faced with living with five years of maintenance and no career to return to. Her ex-husband never paid his support on time, and she had to take him to Family Court on a regular basis. At age sixty, he jumped off the roof of the building where he had his medical practice in Manhattan. His younger wife had left him because he had medical issues which rendered him impotent, and he went into debt to pay for her credit card charges and became insolvent. After the divorce, Rhea moved to Queens, went to school and became a

French teacher, and raised their two children as a single mother. She did not have the time to continue in counseling treatment, but she was able to lead a full life.

Some years after I had treated Rhea, I visited a cemetery in New Zealand. As I was reading the tombstones, I was struck by how many mothers and babies had died in childbirth in the 1800's. I thought about Rhea and her fears, and how susceptible some women are to a fear of pregnancy and childbirth, even today. But what resonated more for me was what a difficult road many women have whether they give birth or adopt, and how strong women must be for themselves and their children.

Chapter Two

Bipolar Disorder:
An Adult Daughter's Struggle with
Her Mother's Illness and Death

"The Best Way Out is Always Through."

Robert Frost

A divorced woman in her fifties named Josie came to see me in a state of extreme grief, confusion and numbness. She was attractive and slim. Her mother, Carol, had just passed away after having suffered through five years of dementia and incontinence while living in an assisted living facility. Josie was an accountant, and her mother had been a nurse before she retired in her seventies. Josie had never explored her feelings about her mother with a therapist before. Her mother's death, and her strong grief reaction, compelled her to seek treatment. She stayed in treatment with me for two years. The following is a compilation of the essence of those visits.

I asked Josie to describe why she was seeking treatment. She replied:

"My mother was an extremely intelligent and creative woman who suffered all her life from bipolar disorder. She was the original 'drama queen,' meaning that she was given to excessive emotional performances and reactions. She died recently, and all of sudden flashbacks and memories about my mother are causing me to feel sad and anxious to an extreme degree. I have isolated myself because I do not want to burden my children or friends with my grief. I have pushed aside my feelings about my mother for many years, but now I know that I must face them or I will be unable to move forward in a positive direction. I am pained to do so because in my religion one is supposed to honor your mother and father, and not to speak ill of the dead. My emotions are mixed. I feel mournful that her mental illness prevented us from being close and from being the kind of mother I wanted and needed. I miss the times when she could be present on some level, although that was so many years ago. And, most profoundly, I feel guilty that I also experience an overriding sense of relief that I do not have to deal with her cruelties and unhappiness anymore. In a sense I am free, but not really. The memories are etched in my psyche, and the post-traumatic stress from dealing with her is lodged in my body."

Over the course of weekly visits, I asked her to tell me more about the flashbacks and memories of her mother. Each week she began to cry quietly. I would hand her a box of tissues and wait. She was intelligent, insightful and self-aware. Her story unfolded.

"When I was a young girl, I idolized my mother. That was probably the time we were the closest. Nonetheless, every day, and sometimes many times within a day, her mood would change and I did not know what to expect. I realize now how traumatic that was for me. I would watch her carefully to see if I could gauge what was happening within her and to try to keep things on an even keel, but life with her was rarely predictable. I never felt that when she looked at me she really saw me. Her mind was always on herself and what she needed, lacked, and wanted. She was never satisfied with her life. On her "good" days, she would take me to the library, read me endless books, create imaginary games with my dolls, and plan fun, educational excursions. Sometimes those days would turn into one activity after another, hour after hour, until I would fall asleep in the car and she would be angry with me for not staying up until we arrived home.

Some of those days she would go on a shopping spree, and buy us whatever we wanted in expensive stores. She refused to buy discounted clothing. When we arrived home laden with shopping bags, my father often yelled because we could not afford her spending. Her intermittent excessive spending became a terrible financial burden on our family. I can remember her doing slightly eccentric things such as washing and setting the hair of my life size walking Patti Playpal doll in rollers, and putting her under the commercial hair dryer we had in the basement. My mother stayed up until 2:00 a.m. most days, and had trouble sleeping and controlling her weight. She would cry for hours if something sad happened in the news. She liked to hear about other people's problems to make herself feel better about her own. She spent excessive time on the telephone, and would talk to people with more words than most wanted to hear. She would buy expensive presents she could not afford which people felt embarrassed about because they did not want to reciprocate with such excess. She would cry endlessly about slights she perceived that others gave her, especially at work, and felt that many did not like her or wanted to compete with her. She would often say inappropriate things to people, such as commenting on their body odor. Nothing was ever in balance.

Outward appearances were important to my mother. She dreamed of opulent fashions, jewels, and expensive homes with lavish interiors. She read fashion and interior design magazines with pleasure, in addition to many novels and newspapers. She would never leave the house without a full face of makeup. She decorated my room with a floating organza canopy over my bed which hung from chains of her own design, and required me to keep my room immaculate at all times. It was a form of her creativity and self expression, but I never felt that she created that environment for me. It was always about her.

Sometimes she was responsible, and sometimes she was not. When I was four years of age, I took a bus each day to a school which picked me up and dropped me off in front of our suburban home. On many days, she was off doing her activities and was not there to meet the bus. I would start to cry as the bus driver insisted that I had to get out and wait for her alone since he had to drive the other children home. He would tease me in front of the other children for crying. When I told my mother that I was scared to take the bus and needed her to be on time, instead of making sure that she was there to meet the bus on time, she contacted the school and complained about the bus driver. After that, the bus driver was determined to make my life a living hell since my mother had gotten him in trouble with his bosses. He teased me every day for an entire year, and labelled me a 'crybaby' for all to hear.

Then there were the dark days, literally and figuratively, when my mother stayed in her bed with the lights out, and could not move for some period of time, or she left the house and did not return at a predictable time. From a young age I knew that I had to take care of myself. I walked myself to school from the age of approximately eight, and came home to an empty house. I had a key and let myself in. None of the other children in my neighborhood did that. Some of my friends and their mothers felt sorry for me. I loved to read and was a good student and dutifully did my homework, so that was not the painful part for me as I adjusted to being on my own. I also had many friends, and I would go to their houses and spend time with their families where things seemed more stable and normal, at least on the surface. Eventually my mother was diagnosed with manic-depressive disorder, which explained many of her behaviors."

I asked her what was the painful part for her. She replied:

"My mother was very hard on herself, and everyone in our household. She demanded perfection, but kept changing the rules about what was perfect so you could never satisfy her, and you could never get it right. Sometimes it seemed that she had a sadistic streak, but she was just as sadistic to herself. She relentlessly criticized everybody. She was overly concerned with physical appearance to an obsessive degree. Over time, I can remember her criticizing almost every body part I had, which made me self-conscious. I felt that I was plain and ugly. For example, she told me that my hair and lips were too thin, my skin was a greenish tone and my pores were too large, my nose was not straight enough, my forehead was too short, my ears were oddly and differently shaped, my buttocks was too large, first my breasts were too small and then too large, at times I was too fat or too thin-the critique was endless. She continually shamed me. She did not like my taste in clothing and told me what to wear. She insisted that I cut my hair even though I wanted it long. She wanted to be the center of attention, but then she would chide me for not being more effusive and outgoing. Even though she would control so many things in my life, I basically ran free while she was at work or at her activities. But when she was home, she ruled me, when she wasn't ignoring me.

In front of other people, she could be charismatic and put on a whole different face, which only increased my sense of shame. If she was truly sick, could she be capable of being that manipulative? Sometimes she acted so fake and loving toward others, but then saved her punishing behaviors for her family, which only increased my confusion.

As I grew older, her mood swings became more intense, her controlling behaviors accelerated, and her criticisms became more frequent. She did not like my closest friends. She told me that I did everything for my resume and did not care about anything. She was jealous of any of my successes, and tried to find a way to dampen my joy.

But what was worse was listening to her speak to and about my father. I had it relatively easy because she did respect my intellectual abilities, although she often said that I had to work hard for everything, and cut me down to size by making me feel that nothing I did came easily. My father was subjected to an endless tirade of attacks every day about every aspect of his being. For instance, she felt that he was beneath her. She had advanced degrees and he never finished college. In her view, he was not intellectual enough or intellectually curious and did not make enough money. She tried to convince me that he was sloppy and passive; that he walked in an ungraceful way; that his stomach was too large and that he did not practice good hygiene. She accused him of not showering frequently enough, although I can never remember him smelling. She said he did not have any interests and that he was boring. She maintained that he never wanted to go anywhere, but only wanted to watch sports. She insulted him by saying he could not fix anything. I never fully sided with his abuser, although she wanted me to.

This was just a brief sampling of the barrage. The only 'compliments' I can ever remember her giving him were that he was simple, but kind, and that he was honest. I could see him dying a little bit more each day until he barely spoke, and just sat and watched television alone. He rarely fought back, and never defended me. I would defend him on occasion, when I was particularly outraged by her behavior, but it never stopped her. She never expressed remorse or guilt about her treatment of us."

I asked Josie for more details about how she felt about the relationship between her mother and father. She said:

"I finished high school one year early, left my home at age sixteen, and never moved back in. It was not a happy enough home for me. In addition to my mother's instability, I was concerned about the stability of their relationship. My mother always confided in me about everything, including topics that I, as a child, should not have had to deal with. When I became a teenager, she began to tell me even more details which I did not want to hear. She confided that she wanted to leave my father and get a divorce, that she did not love him and probably never did, that they were ill suited for one another, and that they no longer had sex. She listed all of her criticisms of my father, which included some new ones I had not heard of. In fact, they never left one another, and they were tortured with one another until the day he died. She tortured herself once she was alone, until the day she died.

Notwithstanding her problems, she was able to be productive and hold down a nursing job from the time I was in third grade until her seventies. Her bipolar disorder was not as serious as some had it, but it did prevent her from being happy, calm and content. I am not certain why she was mean."

I asked Josie about her mother's relationship with her own parents. She replied:

"My mother had a terrible relationship with her own mother. She felt that her mother was cold, critical and unloving, and that the only time she felt loved was when she was sick. She claimed that she did not love her mother, and that any relationship she had was out of duty. I was programmed from an early age not to like my grandmother. But when I thought about it when I became older, I began to understand how difficult it must have been for my grandmother to parent my mother because of my mother's mental illness. Although my grandmother was strict, she was more balanced. My mother claimed that her father loved her more, and that he would continually shower her with gifts which showed his love. She said that her father gave her what she wanted, and her mother was the disciplinarian. When I was eleven, my mother had a terrible fight with her father. She wanted him to lend her some money. He had recently retired, and refused. After that he went traveling overseas with my grandmother. While traveling, he had a heart attack and died. My mother never had the opportunity to make up with him, and she went into a deep depression for a year. She rarely spoke to me during that entire time. I was on my own."

I asked her if her mother ever received treatment for her mental illness. She said:

"I do not remember exactly when she started to see a therapist or was diagnosed. I know that she had a series of therapists. She liked the attention she received, and she liked to talk about herself. To her credit, she always tried to get better and never missed her therapy sessions. My father did not believe in therapy, nor did he trust therapists, and he refused to participate in her treatment. He attended a session with her one time with one therapist, and then declared that he would not attend again. My mother reported to me that the therapist said that my father was passive to an excessive degree. I was never asked to attend any sessions. My father never learned anything about her illness, and essentially was in denial that anything was wrong with her. I think that over time he began to believe that he deserved her conduct towards him, just as I believed that I deserved it. We were not able to earn much approval from her.

Unfortunately, her illness became my responsibility. After her sessions, she would come home and tell me about many things that they discussed. She shared with me that one therapist told her that she was unable to love, and another therapist told her that she was a narcissist. In a way, I was getting therapy by proxy, but I did not always understand what she was telling me, and it was filtered through her distorted lens. When I would try to tell her about my life concerns, her advice always seemed off, and she felt burdened by having to hear about it. She was trying to keep her own head above water. I played amateur therapist with her and tried for many years to help her with her problems by listening and talking to her. She became addicted to my attention. Her outlook on life was very depressing because she always felt deprived, unloved, unappreciated, overweight, and unsuccessful.

After many years of professional therapy, and my inept attempts to make my mother happy, she never seemed to get better, and still cycled with her emotions. She became particularly low during the winter months. When I went off to college at age sixteen, she went through a terrible depression.

I felt I had escaped, but she always made me feel guilty that I left home. I rarely returned during vacations. If I ever had an argument with her, my father always took her side and said I should not upset her. He put me in charge of her mental health, and never was concerned that I might have some needs which were unmet because of her illness.

While I was in college, she had several depressive episodes which almost required her to be hospitalized. She gave me permission to speak with her psychiatrist, and he told me that she had bipolar disorder with atypical features and a personality disorder. She was put on psychotropic medications at that time. Once she went on medication, my mother expressed that she could not survive without it. She continued to take medication from that time until the end of her life. The professionals continually tried to make adjustments of the medication, but she was always 'off.' Sometimes she was better than other times. It did not seem to be based on life events. She never refused to take her medications despite the side effects. She really did try.

From my perspective, I felt that I had lost my mother completely once she was on medication. Her affect was strange, wooden, distant and cold. She continued to make strange and hurtful remarks. For example, when I told her I had an opportunity to teach a class and that it went well, she replied that they were a captive audience and smirked. When I achieved leadership roles, she said the outside world may like me, but my family did not. She always told me that I had no sense of humor, and that I was too sensitive, no matter how hurtful her remarks were. I continued to tell her that her remarks were too critical, but she was unable to change despite my frequent reminders."

I asked Josie how she felt about her mother now. She told me:

"When I was a young child, my mother was the most present she could be for me, but I still felt like an orphan who had to raise herself. I was not able to see her clearly, and I adored her blindly. I can remember some fun times with her, when we would dance to Broadway show music in the living room, and play dress up. We attended many movies and plays together, and she liked my analysis of the characters. She admired my love of reading. However, her illness seemed to get worse over time, or maybe with my exposure to school and other families, I realized what I was missing at home. Over time, I became frightened of what my mother's disapproval could do to me. She was unable to stop being critical of me and of my father. She began to treat me as though I were the enemy the way she had treated her own mother. I was afraid to tell her what was going on in my life because her comments stung so deeply. Many times as an adult I tried to explain to her that she had to be more approving. She asked me why I needed her approval. I tried to explain to her that children, no matter how old they get, still want the approval of their parents. She could not seem to understand that, and, she was unable to curb her behavior.

When I turned thirty, I told her and my father that if she did not stop her behavior, I would not be able to see her. My father said that if he could put up with it, so could I. I knew that I could never cut her off completely. I just did not have that in me. I tried to keep my time with my mother short, limited, and supervised, with other people present, for many years. I knew that I had to do that for my own survival. She was intelligent and manipulative so that many of her mean comments had parts of it with a ring of truth, which made it so painful.

My father developed dementia in his eighties. My mother became even more cruel to him, chiding him continually for not remembering and jumbling everything up. He also lost hearing in one ear, and she attacked him for that. Then she started developing dementia in her eighties, and accused him of having an affair with the home health care aide, and asked for a divorce. She too became hard of hearing. I felt that I had lost my mother again, but I was hoping she would return as a kind person. Each time I visited I prayed she would turn into that person. First her words became gibberish. She had always been so articulate. Then she had trouble speaking at all. She was always giving long, detailed monologues about herself, so this new development was equally troubling. I could not tell how she felt about my father's death. She was so deeply lost inside herself.

She remained unhappy, anxious and depressed almost until her death, a year after my father's death. It was only when she received the morphine drip in her last hours that she seemed to achieve some kind of peace. That drug made her relax. Maybe she was looking forward to being free of her demons, and no longer having to struggle psychically. Before the drip and her incoherence, we told each other that we loved each other. I don't know if either of us believed it. We had been through so much. Some of the last words I can remember her saying before she lost the ability to speak were that she would not be so upset if I went to college now. I was not sure if she meant that she would be able to handle it better with all the years of therapy and medication, or if she stopped caring about me and so would not have minded now. Maybe this was more gibberish. As always, with my mother, her mind was a mystery, and her motivations even more confusing. Maybe she did not know what she was saying all along, or maybe she had the capacity for cruelty which I had trouble accepting? Could it be a combination? Her strong intelligence and her mental illness made a confusing mix."

After several years of treatment, Josie and I agreed that she had completed the work. She worked through her grief over her mother's death, and was able to deal with the complications of her long relationship with her mother. She tried hard to understand her mother's illness and to be forgiving. She felt better about who she was, and how she had dealt with the challenges she had faced in her life. Josie hoped that the next chapter of her life would be happy, fulfilling, and, most importantly, guilt free. She knew that the healthier parts of her mother would have wished this for her, and that even if her mother could not, she deserved it.

Chapter Three

Inheritance Stolen:
the Pain of Being a Sibling

"Brothers and sisters are as close as hands and feet."

Vietnamese Proverb

A woman in her sixties, Ann, came to me for treatment after both of her parents had recently died. She was a social worker, and had adult children of her own with whom she had a close relationship. She had one sibling, a brother, who was still alive, although she was grieving the loss of her brother too, for other reasons. She felt sad, angry, and victimized by him, and articulated that she could not continue to have a relationship with him on any level. It was important to work through her feelings about her brother to give her peace and closure.

I asked her why she felt that she lost her brother. Over the course of her year in treatment, she explained what she felt had happened:

"My parents had a lot of difficulties while I was growing up. They both had many physical challenges including heart attacks, strokes, and many operations between them for a variety of illnesses. They also went through a bankruptcy of my father's business, but they were able to land on their feet. They both continued to work into their old age, and had no interest in retiring until they could no longer work.

My brother is five years older than me. He was very aggressive as a boy, and had difficulties respecting authority figures at school. The teachers would report this to my parents. Although he was bright and did well in school, his conduct was always an issue. He also became a bully with the younger boys in our neighborhood in that he taunted them, and physically pushed them around. The neighbors complained to my parents about him. He had a competitive streak, and always had to win. He liked to brag to others, and was always looking for a fight, which did not earn him many friends. He was also overweight and small of stature, which was difficult for him. When I was born, he resented my presence immediately. As time went on, he felt burdened that he had to do too many chores around the house, but also that he was given the responsibility to look after me while my parents worked."

I asked Ann what her brother's responsibility was for her. She replied:

"For some years, from the time I was about eight years of age, he was supposed to look after me after school until my mother arrived home about three hours later. On the days when he came home, as he had after school activities some of the time, he would go into his room, close the door, and tell me to stay out. He frequently told me that he wished he had a younger brother so that he could play sports with him. He rarely helped me with schoolwork or anything else, frankly.

For the most part, I had to get food on my own. When he was not ignoring me, he bullied and teased me. I have to say that I never really liked him because of all of that. In fact, his conduct often felt abusive. I felt that he was able to take all of his frustrations and anger out on me because I was the younger girl. I was fortunate because I was outgoing and able to make friends easily. He was always jealous that I received many more social invitations than he. Over time, I went to my friend's houses so that I would not have to deal with him."

I asked her if she felt that her parents had a favorite. Ann said:

"I don't think there was a favorite. My father was sports-oriented and so he preferred to do sports-related activities with my brother. My mother enjoyed cultural and educational events, as did I, so it divided up that way. My brother was always making certain that he received his share of the pie, and more, literally and figuratively. He closely watched if I was given something. I never cared if he was. He would complain if my parents bought me something or allowed me to do an activity which he wanted to do. At dinner, he would grab up all the food. I had to make certain to get what I wanted before it all disappeared. It was a continual scramble for resources. We grew up in an upper middle class community, but my parents had a middle class income. My father was a salesman and my mother was an office manager. Although my brother did jobs for money, in high school he also developed a gambling problem, and would play cards with wealthy boys. He always bragged about how much he won, but would never say how much he lost. He bought himself expensive equipment, including a television and stereo, which he kept in his room behind closed doors. It never occurred to him to share those things with the family in the common room, even when my parents had their financial challenges.

He went off to college and graduate school and studied business. His main goal in life was to make a lot of money, and to be able to show people how much he could buy. I could never relate to his consumerism or his life's goals. They always seemed empty and shallow to me. We overlapped at the same college one year and my parents asked him to drive me to school at the beginning of that year. He loaded up his car with all of his possessions, and told me I could only bring a small suitcase for the year as there was no room. He barely left me enough room to sit in the passenger's seat. I was completely encased and surrounded by his 'things.' That about sums up the dynamic. During the year that we spent at the same college, he frequently commented that I did not have the right friends, that I should wear makeup and better clothes, and basically tried to make me feel as though I was not meeting the standards. I was on the Dean's list every semester, and I made many friends with whom I am still in contact to this day. I still wear little makeup, as you can see. I always felt that his criticisms were mean, hurtful and petty.

Unfortunately, over the years, he was never able to make as much money as he had planned, which made him even angrier and meaner. In truth, no amount of money or possessions could probably have satisfied him. He always wanted more."

I asked Ann if she felt that she had been generous to her brother. She replied:

"I never really liked him, so in that sense I was not generous in that it probably showed. Nonetheless, I tried to help him when I could. When I was in my twenties, I lived in a tiny, roach infested studio apartment in New York City. My brother's wife had to get medical treatments, and she had to travel a few hours from her home in another State to get them. I offered to have her stay with me overnight when she came in for those treatments. I shared my bed with her as that was the best I could do.

When I was in my thirties and had young children, my brother lost his job. He had left a steady job, taken a risk, and the risk did not work out. He had a wife and four children. They lived in a different State, and we did not see much of them except at family gatherings with our parents. I felt sorry for him and his family. He decided that he would start a business. He asked me and my husband if we would lend him $25,000. We had a large mortgage on our house, and small children, but we decided we would take out a home equity loan, and give him what he had asked for. During the time period that he used our loan, he came over to our house. He commented that he could never live in anything as small as our house with his family, even though we had five bedrooms and three full bathrooms, with an attic which could be made into another bedroom.

To his credit, he did pay us back, and we never charged him interest. Naturally, he never offered us to benefit from anything about the business. He also complained bitterly that his wife's parents would not give him their retirement money to help him start his business. His sense of entitlement was boundless. What happened later was much worse. When I was in my forties, I divorced. I had a good job at the time. When I called my brother to tell him, he was not supportive. In fact, the first thing he told me, even though I did not ask for it and did not need it, was that he did not have any money to give me. I always spent under my means and saved money, so I never found myself in trouble that way. I just wanted to feel his emotional support, which was lacking. I later thought about asking him why he did not consider taking out a loan for me, if I ever needed it, to 'poke the snake,' but I held my tongue.

A few months after I divorced, I told him over the telephone that I was very depressed and feeling suicidal. He told me that I should discuss this with my children, not him.

Eventually, I moved from my house into an apartment. I offered to give his children some of my furniture, which they took. When one of his sons lost his job, I took him out for dinner, and gave him a list of my contacts to help him. When his daughter was pregnant some years later, I made sure that my contacts at the hospital took good care of her and she was able to get a superior room and extra attention.

I never felt that my brother 'had my back.' He never once came to visit me during that very trying period. The only time I saw him in the year after my divorce was when he offered to pick up me and my children at the train station near his home. We were visiting my parents who lived in the same State he did. He wanted to show us his new house. Despite the fact that he knew I had lost my house and all of my possessions in the divorce, he proceeded to take us around his house to show us every last item he had purchased for himself. He never asked how we were doing. When I told him I was thinking of taking on a second job as a bartender to make some extra money, he told me that they only wanted young attractive girls in their twenties, not me."

I asked Ann how her brother made her feel. She said:

"Honestly, I never felt he loved or cared about me. I always believed that I was a bother to him and just another responsibility he did not want. He always seemed to be the kind of person that had to win at everything, including the imaginary battle he created for my parents' affections. He always had to be the most important. When my maternal grandmother died, he even made a competition over that saying he was the one that was able to see her before she died. He never tried to win my affections, but always wanted to show me that he was the most important in the family. He was competing with himself because I never cared. I always felt it was his problem."

I asked Ann why she felt she lost her brother now, as it seemed as though he was never really there for her all along. She replied:

"During the time period and aftermath of my divorce, my brother unilaterally decided to move my parents from the town where we grew up and where they had many friends, to an assisted living facility near where my brother lived in an-other State. My mother did not want to leave her friends, but my brother insisted. He did not want to do the traveling, and he did not consider that nobody would visit them except me in their new locale. I later found out that he took my parents to a lawyer to draw up their wills and other documents at that time. He did not tell me about that meeting, nor did he invite me to it. He made himself the Executor. He never showed me their wills. The only thing he told me was that I was to expect a certain sum of money when our parents died.

During the next seven years, nobody came to visit my parents except for my brother and his family, and me and my daughters and my life partner. To his credit, my brother did visit our parents regularly when he was not staying down South at his apartment there. My life partner drove me every time, on a regular basis, to visit my parents, and he even cooked for them. When my brother's son got married, I attended the wedding with my life partner. When it came time to take pho-tographs of the family, my brother said that I could be in the photograph, but my life partner could not because my brother said he did not know how long the relationship would last. At that point, we had been living together for many years. When my brother went to Spain on vacation with his wife, he did not even call my daughter who was living there at the time. He never had any interest in me or in my family.

During one of the visits to my parents, my life partner saw some mail on the table. There was an E-ZPass bill addressed to my father. My father was in his nineties, and could not walk. It was already opened, and it had large monthly charges on it. My mother and father had not been driving for years. I asked my brother about it as I was concerned. He sheepishly told me that my parents had given one of his sons the E-ZPass as a gift, and it was his son using it. If the situation had been reversed and my child had benefited, I am certain he would have had much to say. I said nothing. I suspect this was only the 'tip of the iceberg' when it comes to my brother's spending of my parents' money for his family.

My father's brother and his wife invited me to brunch during this period of time. He had been my father's accountant for many years. He volunteered, without any initiation of discussion by me, that I should watch out because my brother would take everything. I told him that I knew that he was capable of doing that, but I could not bring myself to fight with him. He told me that I was a nice person for saying that. I was not sure what was nice. I asked my children if they thought I should take a closer look at anything, and they told me they were fine if I just left things alone. They did not want a big family fight either, especially after my divorce.

My father's death was traumatic for me on multiple levels. My brother was down South. My father stopped eating and was in hospice care in his apartment. My mother was in rehab for a broken bone in a different building. My father had difficulties swallowing, stopped eating completely, and wanted to die. He told me he wanted to 'meet his maker.' I spoke with my father over the telephone after that visit. He told me that 'they' were trying to make him eat and drink. My mother had returned to the apartment from rehab. I told him that I loved him and that he should do whatever he felt he had to do. He told me that I was sweet for saying that. It was as if he needed permission to go.

After he died several days later, my brother made the funeral arrangements. He gave me a date and time for the graveside service. I made arrangements with my job, as did my partner and daughter and her boyfriend. The next day, my brother texted me and asked if we could make the service for the day after it was planned as the cemetery workers had dug the hole in the ground in the wrong place at the cemetery. I checked, and everybody had issues with their jobs and had difficulties in changing the date. He was extremely hostile, and told me that now they would have to bury my father and then dig him up and re-bury him. Five hours later, he told me that the cemetery people were able to dig the correct hole. It was completely traumatizing for me.

At the funeral at the burial site, which was attended only by family members, my brother approached me and volunteered that my father had no money left. I did not understand why he would discuss such matters at that moment. It was as if he did not want to speak to me ever again, or perhaps he thought I would be too weak to challenge him at that moment. He never informed me of any probate of the will. At the grave site, he showed my mother where she would be buried, next to my father, which also seemed cruel and insensitive to me. In his speech at the gravesite, he mentioned everyone present except my partner. My partner had become another son to my parents, and it was very hurtful that he was not acknowledged, again. He told the Rabbi whom to mention, so in the Rabbi's words my partner was not mentioned either.

Not long after my father died, my brother and his wife moved to the South to their apartment for most of the year, and visited with my mother when they were up North. My brother's wife had retired. My mother continued to decline. I spoke with the home health aide who was with her on a 24/7 basis. She kept me informed of my mother's status. She told me that my brother was planning to have the facility move my mother to a studio apartment within the facility. When we next saw her, my mother was in that apartment. There was no room for her aide to sleep there, and she was with my mother during the day. Thereafter, my mother injured herself in the middle of the night and had to go into the hospital. After that she was in rehab, but she never fully recovered.

Some time later, I received a text message from my brother. He told me that my mother failed her assessment, that she would not be able to return to her studio apartment, and that she was moved to a room in the nursing facility portion of the assisted living complex. I was in touch with the home health aide. She told me that my brother said there was no more money, and she would have to look for another job. She said that my brother and his wife came into town from the South one weekend to the studio, and took everything, including my mother's jewelry and my parents' wedding rings. They never told me they were doing that, and never asked me if I wanted anything. When I next visited my mother in the nursing facility, there were no pictures on the walls and no possessions. It was an empty hospital-like room. The bedspread was old and torn. The only thing that was there was the Bose radio and CD player I had given her, and a tray I made her. Other things I had given her over the years were not there."

I asked Ann how this made her feel. She replied:

"I always felt assaulted by my brother. This felt like a rape. On my mother's behalf, it felt cruel that he made no effort to make her hospital room homey, especially since her environment was always so important to her. I later brought her art for the walls, photographs, and plants to cheer things up. On my behalf, it was cruel that he did not let me and my children have anything and snuck up for the weekend and took it all. When my parents were both in their apartment, they always offered that I could take things but I always felt uncomfortable doing so. I took a few little things over the years, but I was not at ease doing more, nor were my children. I do not know if my parents ever made a list of their possessions and who should get them, as I never saw either of their wills. I imagined that my brother would explain what he did to himself by saying he was the one who loved and cared for my parents, and he should not have to consult me about anything.

I asked Ann if she discussed how she felt with her brother. She said:

"I could not bring myself to do so because I did not want to fight. He always needed to be in complete control. If I questioned how he did anything, he would get hostile. He must have felt that since my parents lived near him during the last years, and he handled their finances, that he was entitled to take whatever he wanted to. Knowing him, I am certain he felt entitled.

My mother continued to deteriorate. He remained down South. I then received a text message from him that he was up North for the summer, and that my mother had been moved to the hospital with pneumonia the day prior. I could not understand why he did not tell me immediately. My partner and I went to the hospital. My mother was wearing a DNR (do not resuscitate) bracelet. He came into the room an hour later which we were not expecting. I was upset with him for not telling me about my mother right away, so I did not tell him we would be there. He said that he had been told that she would likely die soon, but that it might take a few days or a week. We sat at her bedside with him for some time. At that point, my mother had a morphine drip and was slowly drifting away. She said that she felt she was fading.

While we sat with my brother, he told us how he had taken forty-six cruises with his wife over the years, and that they were planning a trip to India in the coming months. I was wondering how he could tell us that when he had taken away my mother's home health care aide at the end. He bragged about the multi-million dollar neighborhood he used to live in. I can remember when he lived there and showed me what he called their "great room" and the other features of his McMansion. Nothing had changed. The dialogue was the same. He mentioned that it was sad that my parents both worked so hard for so many years, and that there was no money left. I kept quiet. I was watching my mother slowly die, and this is what he talked about. He made certain he had complete control of all decision making up until the very end, primarily, no doubt, so that he could retain control over the finances. I stayed away because there is no negotiating with terrorists. I felt fragile and alone.

After some days, my mother passed away. Again he made arrangements for the funeral which was a graveside service, only with family. This time there was no problem with the burial. I saw the Rabbi there, and told him to mention my partner's name which he did. Again, my brother did not mention my partner in his speech. He did not consult me about the obituary, and when I googled and saw it later, it did not mention my partner. I felt that his disrespect for my partner was really meant for me. Just as we were about to leave the gravesite, my brother came over to me and handed me an envelope, which, he told me, contained a check. I said that this was not the time or place for it, but he shoved it in my hands. I could not bring myself to open it.

When I arrived home, I took out the check. In the memo portion on the lower left hand side of the check, he wrote "pay off," with my parents names on it. Those words, alone, were jarring. The amount was less than one quarter of the amount he told me that I was to receive when we had the discussion after my divorce. I was shocked. I consulted my children because I did not want them to think that I was throwing away their rightful inheritance. My children told me to just deposit it and forget about it because it was clear that he would never do the right thing, and none of us wanted to get lawyers involved. He never mentioned whether the will was ever probated. I heard nothing from my brother or his wife for months. After the New Year, I received an email from my sister-in-law telling me they just returned from India, and wished me and my family a Happy New Year. I sent back a nice email, but I really wanted to tell her that I hoped she enjoyed the trip on my parents' dime."

I asked Ann why she never confronted her brother all of those years. She said she was afraid of him, and scared of his hurtful words. She knew he would accuse her of being a bad daughter. He always tried to act like an accusing, unloving parent towards her rather than acting as a loving older sibling. He was very strict and unforgiving with her. When his wife's father died, after Ann's divorce, Ann was not able to go to the funeral as she could not miss work. Her brother told her that he and his wife would never forgive her, and that they wanted to cut her off and not have her as part of the family and that she would be all alone.

Ann felt guilty that she did not live closer to her parents, and could not visit them more, even though her brother set things up so that it was difficult for her. She knew that visiting her parents was hard, and she did not always want to go as often as she felt she should, which she also felt guilty about. But oddly, at the end of her father's life, her brother had moved away, and she was the one who was with her father at the end. At the end of her mother's life, Ann and her brother were together for the death, hand and foot, but truly stood apart.

After Ann spent some months in therapy, just by talking about her feelings, she started to achieve some closure. She was feeling less depressed and more sure of herself. We spent some time discussing whether or not Ann would have any kind of relationship with her brother going forward. She did not want to ever see or speak with her brother again, but felt badly about losing contact with his children, which would be inevitable, as she did have warm feelings towards them. She held off making a decision, but knew that she would never be the one to initiate contact with her brother again. In her view, he was too abusive and cruel. For her, it was a lifetime of hurt from her brother, which could not be erased. He had used his feet to step on her hands once too often.

Chapter Four

Betrayal

*"That was how dishonesty and betrayal started,
not in big lies but in small secrets."*

Amy Tan

Over the last two decades, I have seen a substantial increase in patients who have divorced later in life, after their children have 'left the nest.' It is popularly known as the 'gray divorce.' For many women, this can be a particularly sensitive period as they are adjusting to no longer having children around, at the same time that their marriage is dissolving. There are many other challenges too, typically. The aging process has begun, health issues may have arisen, libidoes may be affected by menopause and erectile dysfunction, and some women are sensitive about their older appearances and no longer confident of finding a new partner. Some women had given up their jobs to raise their families, did not have the requisite education or skills to enter the workforce, and faced age discrimination from employers and co-workers when they tried to get back in. Others had given up promotions or hourly intensive jobs to raise their children. Divorce can be financially devastating, and there is no longer time to make up the money needed in old age, with perhaps thirty years of living ahead.

The struggles of one patient, Maureen, is representative of many of the issues faced by this life challenge.

Maureen was an attractive professional woman in her late fifties. She dyed her hair blonde, wore tailored, colorful clothes, and was in good shape for her age. She had a friendly, open demeanor. She had worked as a fundraiser all her life, and had been married for twenty-six years. Her three children were grown and out of the house.

When I first met Maureen, a few months after her she and her husband had separated, she told me that she could not eat, that she could not sleep, that she cried every day, that her thoughts were racing, that she had trouble concentrating at work, that she could not focus to read a book, and that she was more sad than angry. She had just lost twenty pounds. I asked her to tell me what had happened.

"Dr. Mahler. I was blindsided. It was the Tuesday after Memorial Day weekend. Our son had returned home from his first year at college and was sleeping upstairs. We had been alone in the house for the entire past year as the children were grown and living elsewhere. It was 7:00 a.m., and I was in the kitchen packing my lunch, and getting ready to drive to work. I had just had a nice weekend with my husband. We went to an outdoor antique furniture show, and we bought a small dresser for the bedroom.

My husband came into the kitchen. In a very serious voice, he told me that he needed to speak with me about something, and asked me to come into the living room. I had an early meeting and was anxious about being late after a long weekend, but my first thought was that someone had died. I became very nervous and agitated because we rarely sat in the living room, so I thought it must be terrible news. I braced myself. We sat down across from each other. He told me that he was leaving me at the end of August, that it was his fault, and that he was not good at marriage. He had been married and divorced previously when he was in his twenties, and did not have children of that marriage. He told me that I could stay in the house for a year, and that he would move out.

I could not absorb what he was saying. My first reaction was to run away, as I could not face the implications of his statements. I told him that by leaving now, he would ruin my life, and our family. I got into my car, with tears streaming, and drove away with him running after my car for a few feet. When I arrived at work, I sat in my office with the door closed. I had never experienced such a sense of fear and panic in my life."

I asked Maureen if there was any part of her that expected this to happen. She replied:

"For many years, we had been so busy raising a family, performing at our jobs, maintaining our house, working in the community, and so much more, that there was no time to think or reflect. After we became empty nesters, I developed some physical problems including extremely painful frozen shoulders, which required extensive physical therapy, and gallbladder surgery. I was also going through menopause with night and day sweats, and some feelings of light depression. I was focused on just getting through the day at that time in my life.

My husband did not seem to be very happy, but I did not think that it was because of me. He was not very communicative about his feelings. He never said that our marriage was failing or that we should go to see a therapist. The only things he complained about throughout the years were that I did not cook enough and brought prepared foods home for dinner, that I did not drink wine as he enjoyed it nightly for dinner, that I had to go to the bathroom too frequently when we were out of the house, that I was always cold, and that I went to bed too early. Our only real fights were that he wanted more air conditioning and less heat than I wanted in the house and car, and he insisted on reading with the light on in our bed when I wanted to sleep.

I thought he was unhappy because of his job as an accountant, as he had stayed in the same company for his entire career, and never liked it. He had been talking about retirement since he was in his thirties. I had encouraged him to change jobs, but he never did. I was even willing to move to another State to make that happen ten years prior. He could not seem to get the energy together to make the change."

I asked Maureen if she had ever been in therapy with her husband. She said:

"We never went for therapy. I never thought we had marital issues, and he never asked me to. We were a good team as far as raising the family, and taking care of all of our responsibilities. For the most part, we treated each other with respect and did not fight. We travelled nicely together. We had a group of close, mutual friends and saw each other's families for special occasions. After all those years of marriage we no longer were passionate newlyweds, but I did not think that was an issue for him.

I was happy with the stability of family and home, and looked forward to travelling more and enjoying our empty nest. Some months before he asked for the divorce, he told me that half of his 401K had been lost in the stock market crash. He was extremely depressed about it. I naively said that we would be o.k. and that we had good jobs. I did not realize it may have been throwing a wrench into his divorce plans.

Around that time he was changing his will to make his cousin the Executor, which I thought was a good plan and encouraged. At the time of the will signing, he also asked me to sign some additional papers which would have given him the right to move his 401K monies unilaterally instead of having me sign consent as his spouse. He had three of his lawyers in a conference room at a big firm sitting across from me at a table. All of a sudden I panicked and refused to sign the additional papers. I had no representation, but I was smart enough to know that this was not in my best interests. The lawyers looked at me sheepishly. My husband pretended he was not miffed. If I ever had any suspicions, that moment should have been it. But I still hoped he 'had my back' and we were part of the same team. After all, we had a long term marriage and three children. Denial can be strong.

About a year after the incident with these papers, and after I had returned home from work the day he told me about the divorce, I told him that he owed it to our family to go to therapy with me to figure out if the marriage could be saved. He seemed extremely reluctant to do that, but eventually agreed to go to his own therapist, and to go to a couples therapist with me that summer. I went to see my own therapist for a few months before I came to be treated by you.

I could never figure out why my husband would announce his divorce intentions once my son was home from college when he had the whole year to do it. My best guess is that he used our son as a buffer. Unfortunately for my son, he had to watch me deteriorating the entire summer while I was trying to get the marriage back together. I cried every day. My husband had put my son in the middle of the whirlpool, and for that I will never forgive him.

I asked him how long he thought the marriage was failing. He said he started to want the divorce two to five years ago, but that he had been happy for the entirety of our marriage prior to that time. He told me that he no longer loved me. Nothing major had really changed in the past two to five years in our lives, so I was further confused. Our sex life was never the strongest part of our marriage.

Apparently he had worked it all out in his head, but did not tell anybody, including his family and friends. I did not suspect that there was another woman involved at that point, but I remembered that, in the past year, he was on the computer in our den most nights after I went to sleep as I would often wake up to go to the bathroom and saw him there.

I started cooking meals for my husband hoping that if I did that, he would change his mind. I even drank wine at dinner although it made me have acid reflux. Now that I look back at it, they were such desperate attempts on my part, as if changing myself would have made the difference. I found him a therapist who was quite skilled as a clinician, taught, and had written books. My husband went to him for a month, and then his therapist asked me to come in for one session with my husband. Ironically his office was in the city in the same neighborhood where we had lived, happily, as newlyweds. I still had hope that we could work things out, but after that session, I knew it was the end. The therapist told me that while my husband did not have the courage to change his own life by changing his job, he had drummed up the courage to leave me in order to start anew, and nothing could persuade him from that course. Apparently my husband had been planning his exit for several years without my knowing it. I cried and cried in his office. Unfortunately, my husband did not continue for individual therapy for very long. He did not think that he needed it.

At that session, his therapist asked me what I planned to do next. The thought that I would have to work that out was terrifying for me. I told him that perhaps I could get an apartment near my job in the suburbs. He asked me where I dreamed about living. I told him that I had always enjoyed city living, and one issue between me and my husband was that he made me move to the suburbs after we got married. While I had reluctantly agreed to move, I asked my husband to promise to move back to the city once our children were grown, or at least to have an apartment there part of the time. While he promised, his heart was not in that. He dreamed of having a full time cabin in the woods with a dog. Another difference is that I am afraid of, and consequently do not like, dogs.

The therapist told me that perhaps I should think about moving back to the city. It was as if he was giving me permission to live my best life without feeling guilty for not wanting that full-time cabin in the woods. That set me on a course to bring me some happiness. I will always be thankful for that gentle nudge.

We also went to a couples therapist together three times, and at the third session my husband announced that he was no longer returning for therapy. He felt that the marriage was irretrievably broken, that there was no affection between us, and he did not want to put himself through the therapy any more. He had been cold, distant and punishing in all of the sessions. It was if he had turned into a 'pod person,' and that someone had snatched his body. I did not recognize him at all, and wondered if I ever really knew him. He had wanted to be a diplomat when he was younger, and was expert at hiding his feelings, always saying the right things, and pretending that he liked everybody. I never thought he would turn those skills on me. In my view, he had been my best friend.

I mentioned during that painful summer that we had made marriage vows to one another and that our family should be the most important. He said that he did not believe in marriage vows the way I did, and that he did not believe in the nuclear family as I had envisioned it. He told me that all I cared about was the children, and that I did not care about him. That was his feeling. He could not explain it further. I am embarrassed to admit this, but one time I got down on my hands and knees, held his leg, and begged him not to do this. He smirked and said, 'oh please,' as if this was a show instead of real feelings. I realized in the limited therapy that we had together, that he did not know me at all.

Another thing that was a mystery to me was that my husband continued to share the bed with me. We had sex one time after he told me he wanted a divorce, and it seemed like he felt he was cheating on a girlfriend rather than having sex with his wife. Finally, I said to him that if he had no intention of getting back together again, he should sleep in one of our children's empty bedrooms. He seemed to think that I should be the one to leave the bed. I was appalled at his selfishness. At that point I became so upset, I took out our honeymoon and wedding albums, and our family tree which I had framed, and tore everything up in front of him. I threw my gold wedding band down on the ground, which I had purchased, and which he never returned. At that point I felt that he was the most selfish man on earth.

The final thing I did was even more embarrassing, but symbolic. He had been given an expensive, large, glass dog figurine by his first wife for his birthday when they were married. He insisted on keeping it on our fireplace mantel in the living room because he said it was a special piece of art and he liked it. I told him many times that it made me uncomfortable, and that he should either return it or sell it. He said he could not return it because his wife never spoke with him again after the divorce, and he had no intention of giving it back. His first divorce had been extremely acrimonious as he left her, but fought her over money for several years. That should have been a red flag for me. I was so hurt by the way he was treating me, I took the figurine and smashed it on the floor. He quietly swept up the pieces, and we did not speak about it again. I felt better on some level. It was as if I had taken back some power and given myself justice.

During that summer, we tried to go away together for a weekend in the country. I had insisted. His heart was not in it. It felt as if I was pulling a dog by his leash, and the dog would not budge. He was cold and distant. I recall being in the car with him. He was reading me an article in the New York Times about the author, Frank McCourt. McCourt had been married and divorced twice, but it was his third wife, whom he was with for ten years, that truly inspired him. My husband expressed that he was encouraged by that fact. My husband loved to read, and always hoped he would write a novel. He was detailing his divorce game plan to me as if I was some innocent bystander, and in his plan, he had found the third wife who was going to be the charm, and who was going to inspire him to greater heights. In his imagination, that wife was clearly not me.

Then the end of the summer came. Three months had passed since he first announced that he was leaving. I told him that I did not want to stay in the house, and that I was moving into the city and he could stay in the house. I went into the city with my son, we looked at several apartments with a broker, and I took the third apartment. What happened next was humiliating. Although I earned a six figure salary, and had no debt, the apartment management insisted that I get a guarantor for the lease. My husband had to be the guarantor, as I had no one else to ask, and we had to make that a provision in the divorce. I had to get my own credit card, as all of our credit cards were held jointly. One company would not give me my own credit card as I did not have enough of a credit history on my own."

I asked Maureen how she felt about moving out of her home. She said:

"My son had returned to college, my other children were away, and I had to take care of the move on my own. I did not want to ask friends to help, although they generously offered. All of my friends were shocked and said that they never thought that this would happen to my marriage. Nobody saw any signs of discord. I had lived in that home for twenty-six years and our first child was born when we were in that house. All three children went through the entire school system in that community. I put my heart into making our house warm and welcoming. Every room had a memory and some artistic flourish I created. I worked on creating nice gardens outside. We even had a white picket fence, an iconic symbol of an American home. I left everything behind, except what I could fit into a one bedroom apartment, and it was mostly keepsakes from my grandparents and various of my family members. I asked my husband to be out of the house the day the movers came so that I could have some peace during those last hours. The movers finished their work, and I took a cab to the train station to go into the city to meet them at my apartment to start my new life. I cried all the way to the train station."

Over the course of the next year, Maureen remained highly anxious. I offered to prescribe medication to take the edge off for the difficult parts, but she insisted that she wanted to get through it without medication. We went through her divorce together, and we worked hard to put her back together again. It was an excruciating process for her.

One of the biggest challenges for Maureen was that her husband had been thinking and planning about the divorce for some years, and she was at the beginning of that journey trying to grapple with the emotions of it. He was finished with the marriage, was impatient, angry and irritable, and wanted it to be over as soon as possible, and she was having trouble accepting it. She experienced his continually pushing her with the legal process as cruel. During many sessions, I asked her to talk about her process of letting go. She said:

"I had been close to my husband's parents, particularly his mother. I remember her telling me that she wished she had not lived to see this occur. I felt sad for her because she had a solid marriage and was with the same man since high school, and her son had been through two marriages and could not seem to find himself and make himself happy. She told me that she was not going to get in the middle of it, and was not going to encourage her son one way or another, although I could tell that she felt guilty about that decision, at least for her grandchildren's sake. She did not want him to be unhappy, and she somehow trusted him and his decisions. If I was the collateral damage, so be it. When I asked my husband's father if he thought the marriage could be saved, he told me in no uncertain terms that I had best 'move on.' He was a practical man, and knew his son. His parents remain in touch with me, at the very least, for the grandchildren.

My husband initiated the divorce proceedings. He threatened to have the process server come to my office to serve me with the papers. He was not going to give me even a few months to adjust to what happened and to have more therapy to absorb that our marriage was over. He was on his own timeline, and it was not going to take into account my mental state. As my friend, a divorce lawyer put it, he was no longer on my team.

Shortly after that, I learned that he had a girlfriend all along. His pushing me for the divorce so quickly and cruelly began to make sense. She was probably pressuring him to get out of the marriage as quickly as possible, or he was pressuring himself to get on with his new life, or a little of both. It turns out that she was the person he was communicating with nightly by computer for years when we were married. Although he later claimed that they were just friends during that time period, and got together afterwards, I knew that he was emotionally cheating at the very least. I knew in my heart he cheated with her physically. It was obvious that he had made a physical connection with her when I looked back at the signs. She was the person who was going to lead him into his new, supposedly happier life.

What was worse about the girlfriend issue is that I had met her. About five years prior, my husband had a high school reunion. I went with him, and he re-met her then. They started communicating afterwards. She was his age, ten years older than me. I made jokes that he fell for an older woman. While she was physically unattractive, which my friends said should have made me feel better but did not, it turns out that, more importantly for my husband, she owned a cabin in the woods, and had a dog. She smoked pot, tended her garden and make homemade meals. She had a quiet life-exactly what he was looking for. As my mother-in-law put it, they felt comfortable with one another. He moved into her house, which she owned, and gave her money to install a shower and to do other renovations. He told my children he intended to marry her, and that he was giving her a certain sum of money in his will. I later learned that she had been married and divorced three times. No wonder my husband no longer believed in his wedding vows and in the nuclear family."

As Maureen told it, there was a particularly low point during the divorce proceedings. Maureen had stopped speaking with her husband directly. Everything went through the lawyers. The lawyers were negotiating over the last details. Her husband was never known for his generosity, and was particularly tight-fisted. Maureen sent him one e-mail directly. It was several paragraphs long. She reminded him that he had once given a speech to a group about not being materialistic and overly concerned about money, when, in fact, he had spent four years of his life fighting with two different wives over relatively insignificant sums of money which would have made a difference in their lives. He was so outraged by the e-mail, probably because it resonated with him, that he told his lawyer to tell Maureen's lawyer that they would report Maureen to the authorities if she ever sent another e-mail to him again.

After we had many discussions over months about letting go, we simultaneously had discussions about Maureen moving on for own sake. She poured out her heart to me.

"While he was busy finding all of this 'happiness,' I was trying to figure out how I was going to live. I realized that I had been financially privileged during those years of marriage, and that those days were over. My husband made three times as much money as I did. I had taken jobs with reasonable hours throughout the years so that I could balance family and career. From a feminist point of view, I was not going to be reimbursed for that since I worked. It would have been better for me in terms of maintenance if I had stayed home and 'lunched' with the ladies. He was going to get fifty percent of my retirement account. I went to a financial planner to help me sort through it all. He told me what my budget should look like, and it was spartan compared to how I used to live. My husband claimed that he would be retiring in the next few years, so that, too, made me feel insecure for my children at that point. One was still in college. They all had barely launched.

In addition to my 'new normal' finances, my husband had complete control of our monies during the marriage, and so I did not know anything about financial matters. I had always been good with money, and balanced my own checkbook when I was single without a problem. During our marriage, he took control of the checkbook and all financial decisions, and I let him do it. I was happy to cede control as I trusted him, and I had many other things to take care of. In hindsight, I should have been more proactive and I understand that it is a mistake that many women have made. As a newly single person, I had to learn about all of it quickly, and not make any wrong moves as there was no margin for error. This terrified me."

I asked Maureen about what she was doing to make herself happy. She told me:

"I started reading articles and books about happiness, although it was challenging as I had trouble focusing because my anxiety was so high. I decided I had better start doing things, rather than reading, at that time. I tried to remember what I enjoyed doing before I had adult responsibilities. I loved to dance, so I started taking dancing classes. I loved art, so I started taking lessons. I loved to walk, so I started walking five miles a day and working out at the gym. I loved to read, but I was having trouble concentrating on novels, so I went to readings where authors would discuss their books. I loved to travel, so I planned trips, and went with my children."

I worked with Maureen for two years. For the first year she cried at every session. Initially, she did not know if she could take care of herself at that point in her life. She worried about her adult children succeeding in school and at their jobs. She worried about what having a divorced family would mean for all of them. The family had always been close. She had nightmares about becoming homeless and alone, despite the fact that she had a good job, her children were doing well and she was close to them, and she had many friends. She truly tried everything to put her life back together so that she could feel stable again.

The divorce had rocked her boat in a way she never dreamed of at an age when she was feeling vulnerable. Instead of turning to drugs or alcohol, she became intense about health. She ate a vegetarian diet, drank green tea instead of coffee, and tried to eliminate sugar. She started dating, and because she was attractive and outgoing, she was having some fun with that. As we were finishing our treatment sessions, I asked her how she felt about everything that happened now that time had passed. She said:

"I honestly do not feel that you can put a broken mosaic back together so that all of the pieces will fit again. I do not believe that I will ever truly feel stable again, after having been blindsided and betrayed in that way. I am grateful that I am close to my children, and that I have a career. I know activities which make me happy. But I am more like a Catholic or Hasidic woman. I do not believe in divorce, except in extreme cases, such as where there is domestic violence. My husband shamed and betrayed me. I will never forgive him. I will never completely get over it, although I have moved on with my life."

I asked her if she had any relationship with her ex-husband now. She told me:

"I have not seen him or talked to him since our divorce. I do not intend to ever see him again. I lost complete respect for him, and do not wish to be friends. Since my children are now adults, there is no reason for me to see him. My children understand that I do not want to be in the same place at the same time with him. I have encouraged, and they have continued to have, a relationship with him.

My children have spent time with his girlfriend, and always want to tell me about her, primarily because they do not feel she is kind to them. Apparently she has no filter, and says hurtful things that come into her head. I understand that she is not kind to my ex-husband either, and constantly belittles him. I discourage hearing about it, but sometimes they cannot stop themselves. Believe it or not, I am not the least bit curious or satisfied. And when I do hear some details, I react like a mother cub, and that is probably not helpful. I do not know if I believe in karma, but my children told me that he is having difficulties with his girlfriend now and they are going to therapy. They are in their seventies. It does not make me feel any better that he is still not happy. If he had to break up the family, I had hoped that at least it would bring him peace.

I know that he has not finished his journey. When you divorce, you break up more than the couple. There are grandparents, siblings, cousins, aunts and uncles, friends, eventually grandchildren, and on and on. People should not be selfish about their journeys. When you make a commitment you need to stick with it and work on it. I had wanted to mate for life.

One friend suggested to me that sometimes people fall out of love, as an explanation for what had happened. In my world, there are different kinds of love, and once you make a commitment and have children together, you have an obligation. Perhaps that is too simplistic a viewpoint, but it is my philosophy."

I felt I had helped Maureen as much as I could. I encouraged her to continue to take control of her finances. She had acknowledged that she should not have taken her marriage for granted, and perhaps should have been more attentive to her husband to try to find out the root of his unhappiness. Who knows if he would have communicated that to her or if he even knew what his unhappiness stemmed from? It seemed to me that her husband did not really understand her or her motivations, which made him feel unloved. And on her part, she was not paying enough attention. She was willing to take on some of the blame for the failure of her marriage. My job was not to make her forgive, or to forget, or to make her whole again. My job was to make sure she functioned well, was productive, and was capable of finding some happiness for herself. I hope she will.

Chapter Five

Parental Alienation

"The most effective way to destroy people is to deny and obliterate their own understanding of their history."

George Orwell

The Family Court referred to me a patient named Alexis for court ordered therapy. She resided with her mother and sister. She was fifteen years of age, and her sister was three years younger. Her parents had a particularly difficult divorce five years prior, and had been fighting in court over custody and visitation since that time. Originally, the mother was granted custody, and the father was given liberal visitation, but that visitation rarely took place. The three forensic evaluators all agreed that the mother had alienated her children from the father, and that the children were aligned in an unhealthy manner with their mother. I reviewed the psychiatric and psychological reports on consent of the parents, and the court decisions, which were a matter of public record.

In the psychiatric reports, the experts concluded that the father had no evidence of any psychiatric disorder, nor did they find any evidence that the father had attempted to alienate the children from their mother. They reported that the mother had a psychiatric diagnosis of moderate-to-severe Personality Disorder, NOS, with Borderline, Obsessive, and Passive-Aggressive features with the possibility of paranoid traits.

The psychiatric evaluations further indicated that the mother did not obviously interfere with the visitation of the children with their father by overtly denying access on a regular basis. They concluded, rather, that her interference involved a more subtle and insidious form which in many respects had the potential for greater and more permanent damage to the emotional psyche of the children; namely, the psychological poisoning of young persons' minds to turn them away from the noncustodial parent.

What was particularly concerning for Alexis's sake is that the evaluators concluded that the mother had won the war over the children's minds and hearts, and the father was generally helpless to offset that. They went on to say that the father was painted in a highly derogatory and negative fashion, way out of proportion to any possible deficiencies that he may have had. They viewed that as a borderline mental device within the mother's psychology which had been clearly duplicated in the children. According to the reports, the overall prognosis for any major change in the children's attitudes was limited at that time, even with expert psychiatric assistance.

I knew that I had my work cut out for me, but I had an open mind. I was also aware of the potential for gender bias. These were all male psychiatrists who did the evaluations, and I wanted to be careful not to overlook anything.

After all of the turmoil of litigation between her parents, Alexis no longer wanted to visit with her father and his second wife. Alexis remained in therapy with me for five years, and I am sad to admit that she made little progress. I came to agree with the evaluations made by my male colleagues. Alexis never achieved a balanced view of her parents, and had difficulties in her relationships with authority figures at school, and with her friends and acquaintances.

When I first met Alexis, I was struck by how young she looked for her age. She was extremely thin, had white, translucent skin, and looked fragile. She wore clothes more suitable for a pre-teen than a teen, and she wore a hairstyle with bangs which made her look as though she were a girl of twelve or less. She appeared as though she were trying to make time stand still by refusing to grow up, or perhaps her mother did not want her to and that attitude was reflected in her appearance.

In stark contrast to her appearance, when she spoke about her father, she spoke like an adult, and used words that seem to parrot what she had heard. She was disrespectful, hostile, and uncompromising when it came to her view of her father. Over the course of many sessions, and many years, I asked her to describe her mother and their relationship. She spoke about her in loving ways, and uncritically described her as perfect. She felt that her mother had devoted herself to her children, and that she continually provided them with emotional and financial support. She referred to her mother's family as her family, but did not refer to her father's family that way. I never heard her utter a truly critical word about her mother, which was highly unusual for a teenage girl.

During the entire five years of her treatment, she expressed opinions of her father that sounded unrealistic, misshapen and cruel. Her descriptions of him, and her stories about her own treatment of him, often sounded malicious in their quality. She never had anything good to say about him or his wife, and denied anything positive in her relationship with her father to an unnatural extreme. She was extremely bitter toward him. She delivered descriptions of her father which sounded like a negative version of a eulogy or mantra. She never changed the wording of the description, and kept repeating the same stories, which sounded like this:

"My father is a bad father. He is not concerned about me, he is inattentive, insensitive, and has poor parenting skills. My mother never interfered with my relationship with my father, she has not contributed in any way towards my view of him, and she encouraged me to have a good relationship with him. I just don't want to see him or his gold digging wife anymore.

My father is responsible for breaking up the marriage with my mother. My mother told me that my father was disowning us by requesting a religious annulment from her. He stole her family money, and fought her for every dime. My poor mother is continually worried over money. He is selfish and narcissistic. He is always out for himself. He worked too much and did not pay attention to us. He did not take care of me or my sister when we were sick. Even his own brother does not like him. He does not have many friends, and the friends he does have are weird. He is not social and is uncomfortable in public. When he does go out, he behaves inappropriately. When I was younger, he yelled at one friend when she was about to run in front of a car. That was abusive. He always embarrassed me. I am too tall because of him.

My mother was a good wife and mother. She is so lonely now. She does not want to date because she wants to give her children all of her attention. It is all his fault. My father took me on many trips with his new wife, and took a lot of photographs, but those were 'Kodak moments," and did not mean anything. He bought me presents and mementos of our trips together but they were never what I wanted. He did not spend enough money on me, or on my presents, and bought me what he thought I should have. For instance, I asked him for an Apple computer and he bought me a Dell computer. My mother told me to return any presents he gave to me, and I did. I call him by his first name, which he does not like. I refuse to call him dad because I don't think he deserves that respect. He has a big butt, is fat, sloppy, wears funny clothes, and has hair growing out of his ears. He could not fix anything around the house, and he is basically incompetent at everything. His wife is ugly and stupid."

I asked her if she had any discussions with her mother after she had visited with her dad or after trips with him. She said:

"My mother was always interested in everything I did. She put her children first in all ways. When I was younger, she always questioned me when I came home from visits with my dad and that woman to make certain that they did not do anything unsafe or say anything wrong or mean to me and my sister. She would ask where we went, what we ate, and for all details about conversations. I did not like leaving my mother for visitations because she looked so sad when I did. She was afraid for me and for my sister. And my mother would often use my description of those visits to point out things we should not do the way our father did."

I asked her many times why she did not want to visit with her father anymore so that I could get specific reasons. The story was always the same. She said:

"He ruined our lives. I hate him, his new wife, and all of his family. I only feel comfortable with my mother and her family. I do not feel safe with him. My mother knows how to take care of me, but he does not. He kept starting trouble by filing court cases so that I had to go and visit with him. I am older now and I should have my own choice. His wife tries to be nice to me, but I know that she is a big fake and that all she is after is my father's money."

When I asked her for specific instances when she felt unsafe with her father, she could not come up with any. But she did say that any time she had an accident, whether he was there when it happened or not, it was somehow his fault or he did not do something correctly, and her mother did everything perfectly. She could never remember anything mean that her father said to her although she called him mean. There was never any support for her comments. She had an amorphous feeling of fear and aversion toward him. And her complaints, when she was more specific, were entirely trivial. What was striking is that she had no apparent guilt or conflict about her negative views of her father, and how she treated him.

After all the sessions we had together, I was fully convinced that my patient's mother had alienated her from her father, whether her mother intended to, or was conscious of it, or not. Alexis had been severely and perhaps irreparably poisoned against him, and had taken on the mischaracterizations, and misrepresentations, that her mother taught her about her father. She never told me about any instances where her father was abusive toward her mother when they lived together, or abusive to her or her sister in any way, from an objective viewpoint. I am aware of how arguments about parental alienation can be used by abusers in court to denigrate and punish and further abuse mothers, but this was not an instance of that.

The mother's denigration of the father had been complete, and my therapy with Alexis had to come to a close as there had been no progress. The mother had made, and shared with her children, moral judgments against the father's values, lifestyle, appearance, choice of spouse and friends, career and financial and relational successes and failures in life. These criticisms occurred over a lengthy period of time, with different degrees of intensity, but were always powerful.

My goal in the therapy was not necessarily reconciliation with her hated parent, but what I was striving for was a more realistic and healthy attitude toward both parents. But the mother's work had been completed. Alexis's mother no longer had to promote her view of the father. These views had become so ingrained that they had been given a life within her mind. Alexis had lost her emerging sense of self and her capacity for realistic judgment. She was psychologically enmeshed and formed a pathological alliance with her mother against the father.

The literature supports the proposition that only a small proportion of children who have been exposed to alienating conduct by a parent refuse contact with one parent. Some studies show that even where there is pathological alignment with one parent after divorce, in the vast majority of cases, it was temporary and resolved of its own accord, mostly within one or two years. This was an extreme case. Pathological and destructive alienation is rare and hard to achieve.

Alexis had only two visits with her father during the entire five years of her treatment with me. Those visits were brief, in a public place, and orchestrated by her mother. Alexis felt guilty, on behalf of her mother, that she had even that brief contact with her father. She felt almost like a traitor. She then refused to repeat it so as not to upset her mother. She felt no guilt toward the father for refusing further contact.

Alexis kept in touch with me for years. I told her to contact me any time, although we never resumed therapy again. She did see a counselor in college, and later went into therapy again in her mid and late twenties. Sadly, she had no relation-ship with her father. She continued to live with her mother and sister, and never achieved much independence. Her mother did not remarry. Alexis had trouble with relationships, and did not date. She blamed her father for that. She had trouble succeeding at school because she had difficulty concentrating. She blamed her father for that. She later had difficulties with employment. She blamed her father for that.

I consider Alexis's therapy with me one of my greatest failures. I wish I could have helped her more. I am still hopeful that she will get more insight into what happened to her and her family, so that her true family history will not be obliter-ated, and she will no longer need to blame anyone, but can move on.

Chapter Six

Addiction

"Addiction isn't about substance - you aren't addicted to the substance, you are addicted to the alteration of mood that the substance brings."

Susan Cheever

After four times in and out of 'rehab' for alcohol and drug addiction over ten years, Lisa, a forty-year-old woman, initiated therapy with me to help her to maintain her sobriety. She had just been released from an in-patient treatment center, where she had resided for one month. She had no more insurance, her parents could not afford more, and she was told upon discharge that it would be important for her sobriety to continue with outpatient counseling. She was also participating in groups, including Alcoholics Anonymous and their twelve step program, in addition to our individual therapy. I took on some hardship cases without remuneration, and she was one of them.

When I first met Lisa, I was struck by how much older she looked than her age. Her skin was flaky with red blotches, she had puffiness around the eyes, deep wrinkles, and a large belly. It was as though she had lived several lives in her body. She also appeared to be sad, lifeless, apathetic and hopeless. She lived in a homeless shelter and was childless. I treated her over a three year period. During the course of the therapy, I often felt that she was not telling me the entire truth about her addiction out of shame and embarrassment. Because she was an addict, I understood that she would be adept at lying. It took a long time for her to truly open up, and to this day, I do not know if I heard the entire story.

Over time, we explored the underlying reasons why she turned to alcohol and drugs so that we could get at the root cause of the addictions. She suffered from clinical depression, which was one of the contributing factors.

I asked her when she first started drinking and taking drugs. She said:

"I grew up in an upper middle class suburb of Washington, D.C.. My father was a banker and my mother was a homemaker. We had a large Tudor mansion, we belonged to a country club, attended Church regularly, and had all of the material things that were expected in that community. My parents both drank a lot of wine, and my mother also took antidepressant medication and used sleeping pills regularly. My father had issues with depression, also, but he did not believe in therapy, so he self-medicated with alcohol. Most of the members of my parents' families and their friends drank alcohol at social functions. It was a part of our culture. Even when I was a child, my father would give me a sip of his beer or wine, which I considered a great honor. Alcohol was a rite of passage in my family.

In high school, I lived alone with my parents, as my older sister and brother were away at college at that time. I had a lot of pressure from my parents to be friendly with the 'right' people, to be popular, to be good-looking, and to perform well in school.

I was shy and self-conscious. While I was attractive, I did not see myself that way and lacked confidence. I was not outstanding at anything, just average, and that was difficult in my community. I wanted to belong to a certain peer group, which was the hardest to be accepted in. The guys were predominantly athletes, and the girls were cheerleaders and the most popular ones in the school. I was invited to one of their parties at one of the boy's homes in my neighborhood when I was age fifteen, and was offered alcohol and drugs. I wanted to fit in, so I took them. I continued using these substances every weekend at parties for the rest of high school. I found that they relaxed me, allowed me to be more outgoing, and attracted more people to me. I also started to have sex at that time, which made more boys interested in me. My parents did not seem to notice my abuse of these substances, and even allowed me to have friends over with access to their alcohol. They preferred my drinking at home with my friends so they knew where I was."

I asked her if she thought she had a problem with substance abuse then. She replied:

"At that time, I thought I had everything under control. I was only using alcohol and drugs on the weekends. I blacked out a few times, but so did my friends. It was not unusual. The drugs were mostly marijuana and occasionally cocaine or prescription drugs which my friends took from their parents' medicine cabinets. I was still studying during the week, and performed well enough in school to get into an average college, which is where I thought I belonged anyway. I had difficulty handling a lot of pressure, and felt depressed a lot of the time. The alcohol and drugs really helped me with that."

I asked her what happened to her after high school in terms of her substance abuse. She said:

"When I went off to college, I felt vulnerable being away from my family and friends. I was depressed, and I was concerned that I would not be as intelligent as the other students. I did not feel that I could compete on an intellectual level. I felt more confident in my ability to socialize under the right conditions. I found a group of people who liked to party the way my friends in high school did. I continued to drink and do drugs, but at that point I started turning to them every day instead of just on the weekends. I experimented with other drugs, including ecstasy and oxycontin. It seemed as though I was reaching a tolerance level, such that I had to drink more and more alcohol, and take more and more drugs, to achieve the same effect."

I asked her if she sought treatment then. She replied:

"I still did not think that I had a problem. My friends were drinking and drugging. I was able to function and pass my classes. The alcohol and drugs made me feel better, even though I had to take more to get to the same effect. My parents gave me enough spending money to afford the alcohol and drugs. I had a boyfriend in college who used as many substances as I did, so I did not notice that I had an issue. And when I went home for vacation, my parents drank, and they even let me have alcohol with them as they said that I was an adult at that point."

I asked her when she first became aware that she had a problem. She said:

"After I graduated from college, I married my college boyfriend. We continued drinking heavily together on the weekends. He had taken a high-pressured job in finance. I took a job in the advertising industry. In both of our jobs, it was expected that we would socialize after hours during the week with our co-workers and clients. That socializing always involved alcohol.

In my late twenties, I noticed that I was drinking more than most people. My husband did not seem to have as much of a problem. I was finding it more difficult to get up in the morning, and to function all day. I started taking more drugs, which I was able to get easily from people in my industry. I took uppers in the morning, and downers to go to sleep. My depression was becoming deeper and lasting longer. I was not getting pregnant, although we were trying, and that was making me even more depressed. I never thought about the impact of the drugs and alcohol on a fetus. It was all about me."

I asked her when was the first time she sought treatment for her depression and substance abuse issues. She said:

"In my early thirties my marriage started to fall apart. My husband said that I had changed. He noticed that my depressions had worsened and that we did not have fun together anymore. He accused me of being an alcoholic, and a drug addict, and told me that I needed to get treatment. I refused. He started to stay out later at night during the week, claiming that he was at work, and he told me that he had to travel more for work. I started to drink more to compensate. I started hiding bottles of alcohol around the apartment in places where he would not find them, such as behind books in the bookshelf, and behind cleaning bottles underneath the kitchen sink."

What made you finally go for treatment? She replied:

"The fights between me and my husband started to escalate. He told me he would leave me if I did not get treatment. I continued to refuse. He claimed that when I was drunk, and even when I was not, that I was abusive toward him and called him names such as 'stupid, lazy, narcissistic, fat, impotent, selfish' and more. He said that I had gained too much weight, that I was not taking care of myself or using proper hygiene, that our apartment was a mess, that I stopped cooking, and that I was not meeting my responsibilities. He also said that if I ever was able to get pregnant, that the child would be born with fetal alcohol syndrome.

Around that time, I started to 'max out' our joint credit cards. When I was feeling depressed, I would go to an expensive department store, and purchase luxury goods. I would order an excessive amount of items on-line. I had piles of boxes in my closet filled with those items. I told myself that I needed them for my job in the advertising industry, and had to maintain my status. My husband was becoming more and more enraged by my spending habits, and said that I was going to bankrupt us. Finally, he took our joint credit card away from me.

During that time period, we went on a vacation together in the Caribbean. I was drunk during the entire trip. When he accused me of drinking too much, I took everything out of our suitcases, closets and drawers, and threw them around the room in a fit of rage. My ability to control my emotions was completely gone. I told him that he was a 'control freak' and that he was the one who was abusive. By the end of the trip, he told me that if I did not go into a treatment center immediately upon our return, he would leave me. So I finally went.

During the next few years, I was in and out of treatment several times. I kept relapsing. I felt that I could not control my addictions. My husband was more and more absent from our apartment as he could no longer deal with me or my behavior. One time, while he was away, I went through his papers on his desk, and found two plane tickets. One was for him, and one was for a woman whose name I did not know. He was supposed to be on a work trip during that same time period. When I confronted him, he said that I should not be looking through his papers, and that it was a violation of his privacy. I started yelling and trashing the house. He called the police. They came, calmed me down, and then I went into treatment again."

I asked Lisa if she felt that the treatment centers helped her. She replied:

"During the time that I was there, I would detox, and get some group and individual therapy. My insurance coverage never allowed me to stay long enough to truly get better. I learned how to lie and manipulate while in treatment. I would downplay my usage, I would get friendly with other residents who sometimes gave me alcohol or drugs, and I knew the right things to say to the therapists to get out. I really was not interested in stopping my usage, as I felt so badly when I did not have the alcohol or drugs. I also felt badly after I used them. Life had become hell in every direction.

After I was in and out of the treatment centers several times, my husband finally left me. That was a 'wake up call.' I took a turn for the worse afterward. I left my job, and have not worked since. I moved in with my parents and asked them for money, which they gave to me. I stole from them to get more alcohol and drugs, including pieces of my mother's jewelry, silver items, and gold coins. I stole my mother's prescription medication from her. My father was a dentist, and I stole in-dividual prescription sheets from his pad, forged his signature, and obtained more drugs that way. I abused the prescription medications I was prescribed by the treatment centers. I no longer had a moral compass. I would do anything to get the high I felt I needed. I had very few friends left at that time, as my whole life was consumed by my substance abuse. I also stole from my friends when I could.

My parents pushed me to go into a treatment center again, which they paid for. Immediately after I was discharged to live with them, I went to a bar. I drank for hours there. When I left the bar at 1:00 a.m., I was driving their car, while intoxicated, and got into a terrible accident. I crossed the centerline, and had a head on collision. The couple in the other car sustained severe injuries. I was arrested, took a plea at my lawyer's recommendation, and served jail time. After I was released, my parents sent me to a treatment center again, which was one of the conditions of my probation. I also attended Alcoholics Anonymous." I continued to use. My parents told me that I would have to move out of their home, and that I was no longer welcome to stay there while still using."

I asked Lisa how she felt toward her parents at that time. She replied:

"I was extremely angry with them at the time. I ended up living in a homeless shelter. I continued to ask them for money. They stopped giving me money because they were afraid that I would use it for drugs or alcohol, which I would have. They would give me food, clothing, and other necessities. I tried to get money from my brother and sister, other relatives, and friends, but I had exhausted my welcome everywhere. I was feeling suicidal, and told my parents so. I had been manipulating my parents for years and knew how to make them feel guilty, although I really did feel that way. They agreed to pay for one more stint at a treatment center, and then to pay for my treatment with you."

I asked Lisa how she felt about being an addict. She said:

"When I took my first drink and tried my first drugs in high school, I never thought that I would end up this way. I came from a wealthy home, I had every advantage, and I led a privileged life. But despite all of that, I was always in pain. I struggled with depression from an early age, and with feelings of insecurity and inadequacy. I thought that the alcohol and drugs helped me with that and allowed me to do things I did not think I could do otherwise. They made me feel powerful, until they did not. I know that I will always be an addict, even when I am not using. The urge to use was so strong that I was willing to lose my husband, my job, my hope of becoming a parent, my employment, my family and my friends. My family and friends all drank, but I was not able to handle the substances. Maybe some of them cannot either. The rate of substance abuse is high."

We talked for many sessions about how she could best maintain her sobriety. She was very well educated on this point. She said:

"I know that I am supposed to stay away from people who drink and do drugs. I know that I cannot even take one drink, or one pill, or one snort of powder. I know that I must remain in therapy and as part of support groups. I know that I must continue to take my antidepressant drugs and not to abuse them. I know that I am supposed to stay busy and productive. I know that the relapse rate is high, but I must keep trying even if I relapse. But despite all this knowledge, my physical and mental needs for the substances are overwhelming. I want desperately to diminish their power over me. Nobody wants to be an addict.

In the past I felt that it was other people's fault that I was an addict. I thought that my parents set a bad example; that they did not give me enough attention; that my husband was not loving enough and cheated on me; that my family and friends were not generous enough; that my treatment providers were not skilled enough; that my employers were not reasonable enough. I truly believed that anything that went wrong in my life was somebody else's fault. Now I have had enough education to know that I am responsible for what happens to me, and that I must take responsibility for my own actions and reactions.

And yet, I don't know if I can make it. Every day is a struggle. I have to be so strong."

When Lisa stopped treatment with me, she had been sober for a year, she had moved to another city, she was working again in the advertising industry, she lived in a studio apartment, and she started to date. Another psychiatrist continued to prescribe antidepressant medication and monitored her, and she was in various support groups. She maintained contact with her family and visited them on holidays.

After all of her treatment, Lisa had a better understanding of what contributed to her becoming an addict, and what she had to do to prevent herself from abusing substances again. But, unfortunately, self awareness is not all. I hope she will continue to use her support systems to help her remain on track. I think about her and fervently wish that she will be one of the individuals who succeeds in overcoming her addictions over the long haul. I know that it will not be from lack of trying if she fails.

Chapter Seven

Parental Kidnapping

"The abduction of a child is a tragedy. No one can fully understand or appreciate what a parent goes through at such a time, unless they have faced a similar tragedy. Every parent responds differently. Each parent copes with this nightmare in the best way he or she knows how."

John Walsh

A young mother named Melissa, who was in her late twenties, came into treatment with me because of recurring nightmares, and crippling anxiety, and depression. Kimberly, her child, had been kidnapped by the father when she was one-year-old. After two years, the child was finally returned to Melissa, but Melissa continued to suffer terribly from the ordeal she went through, and the aftermath of it. She wanted to feel better, and she wanted to be the best parent she could be for her child, who was suffering also with nightmares, bouts of crying, and aggressive behaviors. Melissa remained in therapy with me for ten years.

I asked Melissa about her relationship with the father before the kidnapping. She told me:

"I married Eduardo when I was twenty-five-years-old after knowing him for six months. We met at a bar in the suburban town I lived in. He had a job as an auto mechanic, and I was a receptionist at a doctor's office. He was born in El Salvador, and most of his family still resides there. He was dark and handsome, he was ten years older than me, and he seemed to be more sophisticated and worldly than I. I did not have much of a family as I was an only child, and my parents were divorced. My parents were both second generation Americans. When I met Eduardo, I was still living with my mother, and we struggled financially. My father had remarried and moved to another state across the country. I did not see much of him, and he did not take an interest in my life. I longed for stability and security.

I was lonely and in need of attention. Eduardo was exceedingly charming during the time that he courted me. He brought flowers for me and my mother when he picked me up for a date. He had good manners, and took me out to lovely restaurants, to the movies, to concerts and shows. He showered me with gifts, including jewelry and expensive accessories. He told me how much he wanted to have a family, and he promised to love and protect me always. He complimented my appearance and intelligence, and made me feel loved and wanted. I fell in love with the man he presented at that time."

I asked her when the situation with Eduardo changed. She replied:

"We married at the clerk's office. Only my mother and a few of my friends, and his work colleagues attended as his family was in El Salvador and could not afford to come. We did not want to have a formal wedding party as we were saving to buy a house. I moved into his apartment, which was above a store. It was one room, with the bathtub in the living room.

After three months, his personality started to change. He became much more demanding and moody. He insisted that I do all of the housework. I was used to doing it, so it did not feel like a burden to me. But then he started to criticize how I did everything. He criticized my food shopping saying that I bought the wrong items and that I did not get the best deals. He did not like the food I cooked or how I prepared it. He did not like the way I folded his clothes after washing them. He did not think that I cleaned the apartment enough. He did not like the products I used to clean the apartment. He did not like the clothes that I wore and insisted that I not wear certain items. He did not like the perfume I wore. He did not like the tone of my voice, my laugh, how I chewed my food, how much I slept, and the temperature I liked to maintain in the apartment. He told me that I did not know how to please a man sexually.

With each of his criticisms, I tried to alter my actions to do whatever would please him, but he kept coming up with more and more hurdles. It became extremely oppressive when he started to criticize my mother and insisted that I not see her much. He claimed that he did not like my friends, so I stopped having them over and stopped meeting them elsewhere.

Then he insisted that I stop using birth control as he wanted to start a family quickly because of his age. Although that was not the time table I would have preferred, I thought that there was some logic to that request as we did not want him to be too old a father. I became pregnant easily, but the intense abuse started then."

I asked her what happened. She replied:

"Eduardo demanded that I stop working once I became pregnant. He said that it was not good for the baby for me to be stressed. I quit my job. At that point, I rarely saw my mother, I never saw my friends, and he had me completely isolated in the apartment. I stayed home all day. He continually called the land line to see if I was home. When he could not reach me, he called my cell phone many times. He wanted to know where I was and what I was doing. He insisted on paying all of the bills from the checkbook, and would give me a small allowance. He controlled the money completely. He bought a stick shift car, knowing that I only knew how to drive an automatic, and was not comfortable learning how to drive it.

When he came home from work, he would criticize me for not doing anything all day. He complained about how hard he worked, and how he had all of the responsibility. He started calling me names. He said I was fat, lazy, useless, and good for nothing. At first he insisted on having sex every day, even when I felt sick from the pregnancy. The sex became very rough, much rougher than before I was pregnant, and it felt like a violation. There were no kisses or loving touches, but just a pounding, as if I were a hole in a wall. I complied with all of his sexual requests. I say complied because it was not enjoyable for me at all. Then, some months later during the pregnancy, he told me I was too ugly, and he did not want to touch me anymore, and that he was going to have to find some attractive woman at a bar to have sex with."

I asked her why she put up with all of this abuse. She said: "I took my marriage vows seriously, and I was pregnant. I did not want to be a single parent. I kept hoping that he would go back to the way he had been when he was courting me. I felt ashamed, and did not want to tell my mother and friends what was going on. I felt embarrassed that I had made such a bad choice marrying him, and, on some level, I felt that I deserved his treatment and that I was not good enough. I kept hoping that I would finally get it right and please him.

The turning point for me came when he started to hit me if I would say anything back to him after he verbally attacked me. I begged for him not to hit me as I was afraid he would hurt the baby, but it seemed as though his need to control me was stronger than any other concern of his. At first he would slap my face. Then, over time, it escalated to punching my arms and pushing me down. Finally, one night he punched me in the stomach and choked me. At that moment I knew that it was no longer about me. I had to do something to protect the baby in utero."

I asked her what she did next to protect herself and her child. She said:

"The next day, I called my mother and told her what was going on. I had been ashamed to tell her before. Also, I did not want to burden her since she had her own problems. She asked me if I wanted to leave Eduardo, and I told her that I did. I was afraid for my life and for the life of the baby. She told me to pack my things, and that she would pick me up immediately while he was still at work.

I packed the essentials, and left the rest behind. I knew that I would never return to that life again. My mother took me to a matrimonial lawyer, and I went to Family Court to get an order of protection against him. I was given a temporary order of protection that he was to stay away from me and my mother's residence, that he was not to stalk, harass, threaten or menace me, and that he was not to contact me by any form of communication. When we went back to court after he was served with the temporary order of protection, he glared at me in the courtroom and denied everything. The Judge gave me a final order of protection for one year."

I asked her if she continued to feel unsafe. She told me:

"I had a final order of protection, but I knew that it was just a piece of paper. I started the matrimonial action, and he used that proceeding to continue to punish me. He threw up every roadblock possible. He violated the order of protection five times by stalking me and telephoning me repeatedly. He spent some time in jail because of it. I gave birth during the negotiations. Then it became a custody fight too. Ultimately, we settled. I was given full custody, and he had a supervised visitation schedule. Because I was so fearful of him, the court ordered that my mother do the drop off and pick up of our child at my local church. I had been attending that church since I was a child. The ministers agreed to the arrangement, and to supervise the visits."

I asked her how the arrangement had worked out. She began to cry uncontrollably, and then replied:

"For one month everything seemed to be going smoothly. My mother gave the baby to Eduardo at the church every other weekend for two hours on a Saturday. The Church personnel would loosely supervise the visit. He was not allowed to take the baby from the Church by court order. On the last visit, my mother and I were contacted by one of the ministers at the Church. He said that Eduardo took the baby, ran to his car, and drove off. It all happened so quickly there was nothing he could do to stop it. We immediately called the police and my lawyer.

I was hysterical. I was still breastfeeding, the baby had never had formula, my mother brought bottles of my breast milk to the visits, but there would only be enough for a few hours. Despite having contacted all the necessary authorities, Eduardo had disappeared off the grid, and no one could find him.

My ability to speak Spanish was limited, but I could converse. I contacted his relatives in El Salvador. One of his sisters, who took pity on me, and was the mother of five children, eventually told me that the baby was safe, that Eduardo was somewhere in El Salvador as far as she knew, and that he was in hiding. Supposedly, no one in the family knew exactly where he was. His family was angry with me for insisting on supervised visits for Eduardo, and they told me that they could understand why he would not want to parent his child that way. They felt he had no recourse but to take the child because of my attitude. Their shifting of the blame, and their inability to understand how he had abused me, made me feel even more guilty, ashamed and alone. Clearly their concept of family was that they would stick together no matter what had occurred.

I learned that El Salvador was not a party to the Hague Convention, at that time, which was going to make my getting my baby back far more difficult from a legal perspective. The Convention would have provided a framework for the United States and El Salvador to work together to try to resolve my international abduction case, but that was not to be. I had very limited funds, and was unsure what I should do. I decided to travel to El Salvador to meet with his relatives to beg them to help me find the baby.

I travelled to El Salvador three times during that two year period when Kimberly was missing. Each time I received a cool reception from his relatives and no information. I hired a private investigator there who was not able to find Eduardo. He would come up with leads, I would become hopeful, and then it turned out to be a dead end. I spent money I did not have to no avail. I contacted every possible agency that dealt with missing and exploited children.

I cried every day during that time period. I was numb, grief stricken, and in a state of perpetual panic. I never felt that I could rest because if I did, I was wasting precious time. I wanted to spend as much time as possible trying to find my daughter. When I felt suicidal, what kept me going was the thought that eventually I would get Kimberly back, and that she would need her mother.

What made me the most terrified was that I feared that since he physically and emotionally abused me, that he would do the same to Kimberly. I did not know what kind of a father he would be, but because of his rage, and need to control, I was not hopeful."

I told her how brave she was, and asked her how she found Kimberly. She replied:

"My entire life was consumed with finding Kimberly, but I had begun to tell my mother that I was giving up hope. My lawyers had done everything they could do legally, the authorities in El Salvador were unable to help me, the investigators did not come up with anything, none of the agencies could help, and I could not find anyone in his family to cooperate.

One day I received a telephone call from a child protective services worker in Florida. She told me that Eduardo had been stopped by the police for a minor traffic infraction. When the police put his driver's license and registration into the system, they immediately were alerted that he had abducted Kimberly. Kimberly was in the car with Eduardo. Eduardo was arrested on the spot. Child protective services came, picked up Kimberly, and they were keeping her with a foster family until I could come pick her up. My mother and I went to Florida, and took Kimberly home. It was the happiest day of my life. Kimberly looked confused when we took her, but she did not cry. She seemed to recognize us on some level. Eduardo took a plea, and was incarcerated."

I asked her if she felt safe now. She responded:

"After Kimberly came home, I continued to have nightmares and panic attacks. She did too. We slept together every night. I installed an alarm system in the house, and was hypervigilant. If I heard a car stop outside, it made me nervous. If the tree branches knocked against the window in the wind, I was startled. I noticed similar responses in Kimberly. Even though Eduardo was in jail, I was not certain if any of his relatives would try to kidnap Kimberly for him until he was released. I did not return to work, because I did not want to leave her with strangers. My mother would give me some needed breaks. For a year, I did not put her in pre-school either because I felt that there were too many adjustments for her. I will never know where she was or what happened to her during her first two years of her life, and that pains me."

After Melissa was in therapy with me for years, she came in for an emergency session in an hysterical state. Eduardo had been released from prison, and had petitioned the family court to obtain visitation with Kimberly. Melissa had lost twenty-five pounds and was again, in a panic stricken state, because of all she had been through, and all she was yet to endure. She told me the status of the court proceedings.

"Eduardo insisted on a trial to get unsupervised visitation rights. I had been interviewed by the Attorney for the Child, who also met with Kimberly before the trial. She interviewed Eduardo as well. A psychologist conducted a forensic evaluation of me, Kimberly and Eduardo and he interviewed my mother, and teachers at Kimberly's preschool, her pediatrician, and some close neighbors.

All the reports recommended that Eduardo be given no visitation, not even supervised visitation. At the trial, Eduardo presented as an angry man, who did not have any remorse whatsoever for abducting Kimberly. The Family Court Judge ruled that Eduardo would not get any visitation whatsoever."

I asked Melissa how that decision made her feel. She told me:

"I felt vindicated that the Judge agreed that the father's taking of the child was child abuse as to Kimberly, and was in violation of my court ordered rights. Nonetheless, I still do not feel safe for myself or my daughter. I live in fear that Eduardo will come and take Kimberly again, or have one of his relatives or friends do so. He does not have respect for me, for my daughter, or for the law. Every time I drop Kimberly off at school, I fear that he may be stalking her, and looking for an opportunity to make contact.

But it is not just about my feelings. Kimberly is frightened too. She cries frequently, and has trouble eating and sleeping normally. She is fearful and tentative. I will always wonder if that is her nature, or if the kidnapping permanently impacted her. When we pass a man in the street who looks like her father, she shudders. She does not play with other children easily, and is withdrawn and quiet. I would like to take her to a therapist to help her to handle her emotions."

I continued to work with Melissa, and I recommended a child therapist for Kimberly. Melissa tried to lead as normal a life as possible, and was loving and caring toward her child. Her mother was a great support to her. She worked with the child therapist as to when she should talk to Melissa about her father, and what she should say.

There are some wounds that cannot be healed easily. I know that Melissa is invested in making the future for her daughter as calm and solid as possible. The threat of the father committing further crimes is real, and cannot be minimized. How Melissa will cope with that threat will make the difference for her own happiness, and that of her daughter.

Chapter Eight

Child Abuse

"Child abuse casts a shadow the length of a lifetime."

Herbert Ward

"I am not what happened to me, I am what I choose to become."

C.G. Jung

I first started treating Gail while she was a college student. She had long, stringy, brown hair which obscured part of her face. The way she held herself, her body looked concave, as if some invisible hand was continually punching her in the stomach. She wore loose, long clothing which hid her body, and sturdy boots which appeared to be her one outward show of strength. She was a literature major, and had a gentle, sensitive quality to her.

When she first talked about herself, she focused on the fact that she could not stop cutting herself, a form of self mutilation. I asked her when this began. She said:

"I started to cut myself with my nails when I was about eleven-years-old, and then it graduated to cutting myself with a razor blade. Sometimes I altered other objects to use."

I asked her if there was a pattern to when she cut herself. She said:

"I cut myself whenever I am upset, pressured, anxious or sad. When I start to feel extremely uncomfortable, the cutting helps to release the bad feelings."

I could never see any of her cuts because of the clothing she wore. After she was in treatment for a while, I asked her if she would show me some of her cuts so that I could see the extent of the injuries. At first, she was embarrassed to do so, but then she modestly lifted portions of her shirt and her skirt. She had angry lines from the cutting on her stomach, upper arms, upper legs, and other places that were not readily visible with clothing on. Her body looked like a war zone. My eyes started to tear just looking at the cuts and knowing the pain she must have been in to do that to herself.

She shared with me that the cutting was getting worse, as she got older and life's pressures intensified, and she was afraid that one day she would "go too far." Nonetheless, she was doing well in school, she had a part-time job at the library, she had roommates with whom she got along, and on the surface, she had made adequate adjustments to college life. She expressed to me that she was interested in men as romantic partners, but she had never had a boyfriend. I asked her about her childhood, to see if I could get some clues as to where the intense pain was originating from. She shared this with me:

"I grew up in a middle class home in a rural area. My mother worked as an aide at the local elementary school, and my father drove a school bus. I had a sister who was three years younger. I remember feeling secure and happy with our family unit. All of that changed for me when I was eleven-years-old. My paternal grandmother died, and my paternal grandfather came to live with us. They lived in another state, so we only saw them once a year, Christmas time, before that. They gave us presents, and treated us well. I never spent much time with my grandfather, but I had warm feelings toward him.

My grandfather once owned a highly successful construction business. He had a farm where he grew Christmas trees as a retirement business while my grandmother was still alive. He was a large man, with enormous hands and feet. He seemed lost in our house, with not much to do, and he appeared to be grieving the loss of my grandmother. His loneliness was palpable. I noticed that he drank a lot of alcohol. My parents both worked full-time, so our grandfather, in effect, became our babysitter from the time when my sister and I got home from school until the time my parents came home. He would often babysit at night for us if my parents went out.

At first it was comforting to have him living at our home. Initially I thought he was being kind and I trusted him. He gave us special candy treats. He was a woodworker, so he made wooden toys for us. He helped us with our homework. He started to give me extra money. He bought me special presents, such as jewelry, and my favorite chocolates. He even picked flowers for me. He gave me more attention than my sister. I thought he liked me more. I did not realize that he was giving me extra regard as a manipulation.

My parents were out of the house a lot. Having the attention from him felt satisfying. But over time, he started to make some demands which made me feel increasingly uncomfortable. He insisted that my sister and I kiss him on the lips when we came home from school and before we went to bed. When he would read to me, he insisted that I sit on his lap, and he moved me around on his penis until he got an erection. When I was taking a bath, he came into the bathroom, and insisted that he wash me in my private parts, and then he sat me on his lap and dried me. Sometimes when I was changing, he came into my room so that he could see my nude body. I tried to cover up, and then he pulled the towel away so that he could gaze more.

Sometimes I watched television with him. He started to have me watch pornographic channels with him. He put a blanket over the two of us, and he made me rub his penis.

By the time I was twelve, I had started to develop breasts. When my parents were out, he came into my bedroom at night when he thought my sister was asleep, and started to fondle my breasts and kissed me on the lips. Eventually it accelerated, and he started to rub my vagina and to stick his finger in it. I asked him to stop, and he told me that there was nothing wrong with it, that he loved me, and this was a way to show his love. When my body started to respond, despite what I was feeling about it, he said that I made him do it and wanted him to do it. He said that he raised animals on his farm, and all of this was perfectly natural. He made me rub his penis until he ejaculated. Sometimes he would masturbate and make me watch. He told me to never tell anybody what we did together as it was our secret. He said that I enjoyed it as much as he did, and he was happy for that. He said that I teased him and made him do these things to me. He told me that I dressed provocatively just to arouse him. He said he was lonely, and needed to feel loved that way. I felt scared, and angry with him, but I also felt some tingling from it, and I felt guilty about that.

Eventually he started to come into my room regularly, and he put his penis in my vagina each time. The first time it hurt and I bled, but after that it did not. I looked up at the ceiling at a crack, and pretended I was not there until it was over. I learned how to numb myself. This went on until I was fourteen. My grandfather discouraged me from having boys over to the house and from going to parties. I guess he did not want any competition."

I asked Gail if she told anyone what was going on. She said:

"At first I was not sure if what he was doing to me was wrong. But as he accelerated what he did to me, I knew it was not right. I loved and trusted him. It was hard to face the truth. When my friends started talking to me about their sexual experiences with boys, and I learned things in health class, I realized that my grandfather was treating me like a wife. I was too embarrassed to tell my friends, and my sister did not fully realize what was happening to me because he would come into my room while she was sleeping. I was afraid that he would start doing the same things to her, but he did not seem to have the same sexual interest in her. I felt tainted, and I did not want her to feel that shame. My silence felt like a betrayal of her, which increased my feelings of guilt.

I was afraid to tell my parents and anyone else in our extended family. My grandfather was a decorated World War II veteran. He was respected and loved by my entire family as he came from humble origins, and became a successful businessman. He was the patriarch of the family, and helped everyone out financially. He gave my parents a lot of money while he was living with us, which helped to ease their burden. I was scared that my parents would not believe me, or they would blame me for what happened. And without my grandfather's financial support, life would be much more difficult for them.

Eventually, when I was fourteen, I missed my period. I was scared that my grandfather made me pregnant, although that was probably unlikely due to his age. I felt that I had to tell my mother what was going on, in any event."

I asked Gail what happened when she told her mother. She said:

"At first my mother said it was not possible. She asked me for details, which I gave to her. She told my father, and he hit me. He said I was lying. He said that I was having sex with boys at school and just did not want to admit it, and that it was not possible that my grandfather would ever do such things. My parents started to fight, and I thought that I had caused them to want to divorce. I did not know what to do. Eventually I told the school nurse, because I wanted to find out where to get an abortion. Soon after that I got my period. I had not been pregnant. The nurse made a report to the police about my grandfather's sexual abuse of me. The District Attorney decided to prosecute. My father asked my grandfather to move out of our house and to go live with his brother. After that, my father never looked me in the eye again. He held me responsible for breaking up the family."

I asked her what happened with the criminal proceeding. She said:

"My grandfather pled not guilty, but then, when his attorney learned that I would testify, and that we had some evidence (I had kept some semen soaked bed sheets for testing) he apparently talked my grandfather into taking a plea. I was spared having to testify against him at trial. My grandfather served time in prison, but died of cancer while incarcerated. My parents ended up divorcing because my mother came to believe me, but my father could not. My grandfather never apologized to me about what he did. I think he felt it was his right to take what he wanted, and he deluded himself by thinking that I wanted to have sex with him too."

I asked Gail how she felt about the legal proceedings. She said:

"Even though I know that I was luckier than most victims in that the court system brought my grandfather to justice, I still felt that the legal process was brutal. I had to repeat what happened to me to so many people. I had to face my grandfather in court at numerous proceedings. The Prosecutor carefully questioned me about my story, which sometimes made me feel that he did not believe me. I did not have the support of my family while I was going through the proceedings. My grandfather was an older man, and I felt guilty that he had to serve time in prison. Somehow, it did not feel like a win to me."

I asked her how she felt about her parents. She said:

"My mother felt guilty for not protecting me from my grandfather's abuse, but said she had no idea what was going on. She was so busy working, and when she was home, my grandfather hid all of his behaviors from her. She also felt guilty that we did not have the kind of relationship where I felt comfortable confiding in her earlier. She was depressed that she was divorced, and on some level does blame me for that. To this day, she has a hard time discussing the abuse with me. She sometimes says things which make me think that a part of her does not want to believe me. I never felt solid support from her. I wish she could do more to support me emotionally. The fact that I had to tell a nurse at school tells you something about our relationship. I am not gratified that she left my father over it because she is not doing well mentally or financially.

Our whole family is ripped apart. My father will not talk to me anymore. He lives with his brother. He does not believe that his father could do such a thing, and he called me a lying whore many times. My father and I were never close, but we had a loving relationship. The fact that I lost him in all of this is beyond painful. I have tried many times to understand why he won't believe me. I know he loved his father very much, and cannot bear to see him in a negative light. But it makes me angry that he did not want to do more to protect me and to protect my sister. We were the innocents. We were the ones who needed his help. I have lost a lot of respect for him, and I do not know if I can ever forgive his reactions, although I think I understand them.

My father's entire family took my grandfather's side. They believed him one hundred percent when he denied everything I said. My father insisted that I had a vivid imagination, and just wanted to cover up for my loose relationship with boys. After my disclosure of the abuse, nobody on my father's side of the family let me attend their gatherings or go to their homes. This contributed to my feeling of being 'spoiled goods.' When I went home from college for the holidays, my mother was the only one who had me to her home where she lived with my sister."

I told Gail that I understood how painful these losses must have been for her. I asked her if she ever discussed what happened with her sister. She replied:

"My sister and I shared a bedroom. I thought she was asleep when my grandfather came into the room at night. Apparently that was not always the case as my sister told me, after my grandfather was in prison, that sometimes she heard my grandfather's grunting noises. She would pretend to be asleep. I asked her why she did not say anything to me, and she said she was ashamed for me, and afraid that he would do it to her. She said that as she was getting older, my grandfather was starting to give her more presents, and to touch and kiss her too. She was afraid of my grandfather, and afraid that our father would not believe her. She did not want to lose our father's love. She did not want to report our grandfather to the authorities because of that.

She told me that her silence all those years made her feel guilty. In that sense she felt she had been abused as much as me, and she expressed that she will never forgive herself for not protecting me even though she was the younger one. We cried about it together many times. My sister had an eating disorder, which was her form of self-punishment. She started to gamble in high school, and had a full blown addiction to it. I think she used those addictions as her coping mechanism. She still lives with my mother, and has lost a lot of money which she does not have. She remains an anorexic. I have encouraged her to go to therapy, and I hope that she will. I have spoken to my mother about it."

After many months of therapy, I asked Gail why she thought she cut herself. She said:

"I had to find some outlet for my intense emotions just as my sister did. I felt like a victim. I could not control what my grandfather did to me. I loved my grandfather, and trusted him. He took away my innocence and used me for his own needs and gratification. He manipulated me, and tried to make me feel that I was causing him to want me sexually. I was too young at the time to understand what he was doing. It was as if I was a zombie. I pretended that what he was doing to me was not really happening. I floated above it and disassociated myself from it. That saved me from having to truly face what was happening. I now know that he raped me over and over. Even though I know from my therapy that it was not my fault, I still feel intense shame.

My father's inability to believe me caused me such intense pain, it is hard to even describe. By cutting myself, it eased my psychic pain, and focused me on my physical pain instead.

When my father rejected me, and his entire side of the family ostracized me, it was as if I had been victimized all over again."

After many years of therapy, I asked Gail if she had a boyfriend. She said:

"I have had a difficult time socializing with men. I am so ashamed about what happened to me. I am afraid that if a man found out, he would not want to go out with me. I feel as though I am tainted goods and that no one will ever accept that I was raped by my grandfather. I feel dirty and hate my body. If I get aroused watching a movie, it makes me feel dirty because it mimics a feeling I had with my grandfather. I did not date at all while I was in high school. While in college, I went to some parties and had too much to drink in order to feel comfortable. At one of the parties, a man started kissing and fondling me. I started to have flashbacks about my grandfather, and quickly left the party. Now that I am out of college, working, and living with roommates, I still do not date. I am afraid that I will never be able to have sex with a man without being traumatized. I am afraid that I will never be able to have a normal relationship, sex, and a family. I am ashamed of the cut marks on my body.

What is also painful for me is that I no longer trust people. If someone is kind to me, I automatically think that they want something from me. I no longer trust authority figures. I had seen college professors flirting with their students, and it reminded me of what happened to me with my grandfather. At work, an older man who has his desk near mine leers at me and makes sexual remarks. I say nothing. I do not trust my ability to distinguish people who are ethical from those who are not. I was so passive with my grandfather for so long, I am afraid that I will accept however anyone wants to treat me, even if they are abusive."

I asked Gail about how she was feeling about her group therapy. She said:

"As you know, while I have been in therapy with you, I have been attending a group with other victims of sexual abuse. I have listened to their stories, and I know I am not alone. So many of us face the same struggles going forward. We cannot erase what happened to us. We are trying to figure out a way to accept what happened to us. We are trying to feel better about ourselves and not to self-blame. Some of us turn our anger against others. Some of us turn our anger inwards. I do the latter. My cutting myself is so I won't cut anyone else. The group is a safe place for me to express myself.

A few of the people in our group have shared how they sexually abused others after they were abused, and how guilty they felt about that. I do recall that while I was in middle school, I did touch some of the neighbor children in the ways in which my grandfather touched me, even though they did not want it. I hope that I did not scar them too. That did not go on for very long as something inside me said it was not right and I stopped.

Some of the people in my group abuse substances. Others are sexually promiscuous. There are many forms of addictions which abuse survivors use to cope. We are trying to learn healthier ways to manage our complex emotional responses. It is so difficult.

At this point in my therapy, I understand what happened to me with my grandfather. For the most part, I forgive myself because I know that I was a child, and it was not my fault. But I struggle with being kind to myself. I still want to punish myself about it. While I am cutting myself much less, I have not stopped completely."

We discussed how she could become more compassionate toward herself. We talked about how it is a process, and acknowledged that she is on her way with it. We talked about how she could take better care of herself. She kept a journal to express her feelings, and to record when she cut herself, and why. It helped her to control those urges. She communicated with her mother and sister on a regular basis, and they continued to discuss what had happened in their family, which was a comfort to Gail. She continued in her group therapy, as she felt that only people who went through what she did could really understand all of the facets to it. She reached out to her father and members of his family, but they continued to reject her, and she realized that there were some aspects of what had occurred which no effort on her part could repair. She stopped blaming herself for that.

Ultimately Gail became a social worker, and began to work with victims of child abuse. In addition to becoming kinder to herself, she was able to bring that compassion toward others who were suffering. It became a calling for her, and it was as helpful to her as it was to the people whom she nurtured. Her ability to understand what they went through was a gift. She is choosing what she wants to become, rather than being defined by what happened to her.

Chapter Nine

Teen Dating Violence and Revenge Pornography

"Abuse is NOT love. Abuse is about control."

Domestic Violence Survivor

As part of my practice, I took on some clinic patients. It was gratifying for me because I did not want income to restrict the people whom I could help. Aiesha was a black girl, age sixteen, who lived in an inner city project with her grandmother and two siblings. The family survived on welfare payments. Her mother was a crack addict, and although she technically lived with the family, she would disappear for days, months, and even years. Aiesha never knew her father. He was also a drug addict, and did not have much of a relationship with her mother when she became pregnant.

Aiesha's grandmother did her best to hold the family together, but she was getting older and was not in the best of health. Her grandmother was active in her Church, and tried to give her grandchildren a sense of community. Her grand-mother, her Church, and her school gave Aiesha the only sta-bility she ever knew. What helped Aiesha to stay grounded was her love of reading. Her time spent in the school library was a safe and comforting place for her. She had a few close friends, and spent most of her time between home, school, and Church. Her grandmother made certain that Aiesha was not out at night, and encouraged her to do her homework.

Aiesha was referred to me by her school psychologist as she needed more treatment than the school could provide. When I first met her, I was struck by how shy and withdrawn she was. Her hair was in an Afro style, and she carried herself with her back straight and with much dignity. She shared with me that she was suffering from what had occurred with her ex-boyfriend, and was having trouble functioning at school because of it. I asked her what happened. She told me:

"I have always felt scared and alone. My mother, when she lived with us, would bring home men who frightened me. They physically assaulted her in front of me and my siblings. One of her boyfriends threw me to the ground and kicked me when he was smoking crack. When my mother was present it was a night-mare. Then she would disappear for long periods of time. She was always high on drugs, which made her behavior erratic. Some-times she was loving toward us, and other times she was raging. My grandmother tried to protect us, but she had a lot of physical illnesses, and raising three grandchildren at her age was difficult.

When I turned fourteen, I met an older boy in his early twenties named Darnell. He lived in the projects with his grandmother as well. He had finished high school, and had been working in a local restaurant for a few years. Unlike me, he did not do well in school and did not like to read. He was handsome and seemingly confident. He walked with a swagger, and wore expensive clothes and sneakers. I never thought someone like him would be interested in me. At first he started walking me home from school on occasion. I liked the attention and my girlfriends were a bit jealous. Then he insisted on walking me home every day.

When we weren't together, he would text me many times in a day. He wanted to know where I was and who I was with every minute. In the beginning, it made me feel happy, because no one ever seemed to care about me as much as he did. He had a full time job, and would buy me whatever I wanted. If I needed clothes, he would get them for me. He treated me to food, and paid for the movies and other types of dates. He said that I belonged to him, and he would protect me. When he came to my apartment, he would talk to my grandmother, and bring presents for my younger brother and sister. He told me that since I was smart and did well in school, that I was going to be a success. He made me feel that I could accomplish anything. My grandmother was not happy that I was dating an older boy, but Darnell charmed my grandmother. She was pleased that I was not running with a wild group and doing drugs like my mother did at that age.

Although I was not really ready to have intercourse, he told me that I was the one for him, that he would marry me someday, and that there was no reason for us to wait to express our love. We had sex without protection, and he said he wanted me to get pregnant so that everyone would know that I was his woman. He took some nude photographs of me on his cellphone. He told me that they were just for him to look at when he was not with me since he always missed me so much when we were not together.

If we went to a party, he made certain that I did not talk to any other boys. After we had been dating for about six months, we went to a party at another apartment in the projects. A boy named DeShawn, whom I knew since we were children, was there. We started talking with one another. Darnell insisted that we leave the party early, even though I was having a good time. On the walk home, Darnell started yelling at me. He accused me of flirting with DeShawn, and called me a slut. When I tried to explain that I knew DeShawn for many years, he accused me of having had sex with him. He pulled my hair, punched me in the face, and threw me to the ground. He kicked me in my stomach repeatedly. He told me that no woman of his was going to disrespect him. He grabbed my cell phone and demanded to know the password. He scrolled through my text messages to see if he could find anything. I cried and cried. From then on, he checked my cell phone every time we were together and tracked wherever I went.

The next day, he came to my apartment with a mix of some songs that I liked. He said he was sorry, and that it would never happen again. He told me that he loved me so much, and that it pained him to think of another boy near me. I wanted to believe him, so we made up. I started to question myself and thought that perhaps I was flirting with DeShawn and that I deserved to be called on it. Also, I had witnessed my mother beaten by and screamed at by some of her boyfriends. I was not certain if that was part of growing up."

I asked Aiesha if she knew that what Darnell did to her was wrong. She said:

"I read a lot of books. I knew that not everyone lived the way my family did. I had no role models in real life to show me what a good relationship between a man and woman looked like. I had attended a mandatory teen dating violence workshop at my school, so I knew in my heart that something was wrong with my relationship with Darnell.

I knew, also, that I did not want to get pregnant. I went to Planned Parenthood, and they gave me some birth control pills. When Darnell found out that I was taking them, he beat me severely, and told me that I should never disrespect him again if I wanted to live. He told me that if I told anyone what he did, he would kill me.

Nothing much occurred with Darnell for a few weeks after that incident. We saw each other daily, and he did not do anything unkind. Then one day he came to my school, and saw me standing with a group of boys and girls on the side-walk. We were talking and laughing. He came over, grabbed me roughly, and walked me home. He again told me that I was a slut, and accused me of having sex with other boys. He had a deadly look in his eyes, and started to choke me until I felt that I would black out. I was never so terrified in my life. The way he choked me, he left no outward marks, but he had crossed a new line.

His violence toward me and his threats were intensifying. When he beat me, he had a dead look in his eyes as if he was not really seeing me. When he would later come to me for forgiveness, he would act like a little boy. He put his head on my lap, cried, and begged me to stay with him. He said that he did not mean to hurt me, but he did not want me to disobey him. Our relationship always improved after a beating, but then something else would trigger him again, and the cycle would start over.

After a particularly bad fight, he posted nude photographs of me on the internet which he had said he was going to keep private. That was the ultimate revenge. Everyone in the school saw them and many students made comments to me the next day. I was a shy, quiet girl, and there was no greater shame for me than that. Darnell finally took the photographs down, but the damage had already been done, people had shared them, and they can never be fully erased from the internet. He told me that he would put the photographs up again if I did not listen to him. I learned from one of my friends that this was called revenge pornography, and that Darnell could be in legal trouble for doing that. At that point, my friends started to become concerned for me and they wanted to know what was going on. I was not ready to confide in them yet as I was still too embarrassed."

I asked Aiesha when she decided to tell the authorities about how Darnell was treating her. She told me:

"I was able to hide the scraps and bruises pretty well. Darnell mostly beat me where nobody else could see it. My grandmother started to notice the injuries, as she saw me in my underwear, and asked me how I got the scraps and bruises. I claimed that I fell off of my bicycle. For months I was too ashamed to tell anyone what was really going on. I was supposedly a smart girl who should know better. I was also deathly afraid that he would actually kill me if he found out I told anyone.

Then one day I nearly fainted in class and was taken to the school nurse. She examined me and saw all the bruises and cuts. She was a very sympathetic, sweet person, and I opened up to her and told her what was going on. I had reached a breaking point, and I almost did not care what happened to me. She told me that I was a domestic violence victim. I never thought of myself that way, and started reading about it. She reported the incidents to the police, to other school authorities, and she told my grandmother."

I asked her how her grandmother reacted when she heard about what Darnell had been doing to her. She said:

"My poor grandmother felt so badly. She cried and cried. She told me that she loved me, and that she felt guilty that she had not noticed anything sooner. She blamed herself that she had accepted my lame explanation about the bicycle accident. She asked me why I did not tell her sooner, and I explained how ashamed I was and that I almost felt like I deserved Darnell's treatment. She told me that she would do everything she could to support me and to get me out of the mess. She told me that no one deserves what Darnell did to me. It was hard to believe that my mother had been raised by such a wonderful, wise woman. I wept in gratitude that at least I had my grandmother on my side.

Then I obtained an order of protection against Darnell. My grandmother accompanied me to court. I did not want to bring further criminal charges against him, and I told the District Attorney's Office that I would not testify. Despite the order of protection, Darnell continued to stalk me. I looked out of the window of my apartment, and I saw him standing outside looking up at my window all hours of the day and night. He followed me home from school, and he showed up at the supermarket, the Church, and the library. Sometimes he followed me while he was in his car and I was on foot. He drove in a way that made me feel that he would run me over.

He came to my apartment and left presents outside the door, and pushed notes under the door. When I ignored him and did not respond, I found a dead rat outside the door, which I thought he left.

He sent me hundreds of texts begging me to come back to him. He further harassed me by calling my cell phone day and night. He left long, angry messages with many threats. He also cried in the messages and told me he forgave me for going to the police. He had his friends contact me. They told me that I was ruining his life and his future, and that if I participated in a criminal prosecution I would be in trouble with all of them.

I did not want to file violations of the order of protection because I was scared that the violence would escalate.

When Darnell realized that I was not going to have a relationship with him ever again, he started to text me with threats about hurting my grandmother, brother and sister. I realized that he was more desperate and dangerous than I had anticipated, and that I would have to take action. I told my grandmother, and went to the nurse and confided in her. She referred me to the school psychologist, and I also went to a center for battered women to learn about my rights and to figure out next steps. I spoke with lawyers there, and they helped me to understand the legal process.

Darnell was arrested, he pled guilty to multiple charges, and he is serving prison time. While in prison, he has written me long letters, which he sent to his friends to give to me, although he is not supposed to contact me. He claimed that he still loves me and that when he gets out of prison, 'we can be together again.'"

I asked her if she is still afraid of him now that he is in jail. She said:

"I am terrified of him. Nothing seems to stop his behavior - not an order of protection; not a criminal prosecution; not jail time. I wonder if I will have to worry about his finding and hurting me and my family in the future. I am worried for myself and for my grandmother and siblings. This anxiety is crippling me at school and in everything I do."

We spent many months talking about her fears, how to best calm them, and how to take care of her body and mind. She was accessing many resources for domestic violence victims in the community to help her as well. We also spent time discussing how she could prevent herself from ever becoming a victim again. She began to understand her needs, and healthier places to fulfill them. The other challenge was her poverty. She was getting help from the school to access scholarships and loans for community college. She was an intelligent girl who just needed opportunities to achieve her independence.

Darnell was the wild card in all of this. Despite all of her best efforts, if he remained obsessed and fixated on her, it would be something she might have to deal with for a long time. All one can do is prepare tools. She is now well equipped.

Chapter Ten

Toxic Family

*"All family life is organized around the most
damaged person in it."*

Sigmund Freud

"I looked up my family tree and I found out I was the sap."

Rodney Dangerfield

Olivia, a businesswoman in her fifties, became my patient
after she started to have heightened anxiety, primarily due to
difficulties with her sister, Mia. Her parents had died some
time ago, and Mia, who was seven years younger, was her only
blood family left.

Olivia was divorced, and had been living with Tibor for
the past ten years. While she never gave birth to children, she
had a loving relationship with Tibor's two grown children. She
had a full professional life, owned her own tech company, and
was extremely successful financially. Olivia had surrounded

herself with many wonderful friends dating back to her child-hood. She kept adding more special people as the years went on. Her relationship with her sister, however, was causing her enormous amounts of pain, and she needed to talk about it with a professional so as not to unduly burden her friends.

I asked Olivia to describe what it was like growing up with Mia, so that I could have a sense of their shared history, and a better understanding of the roots of their relationship. Olivia told me:

"Our parents were originally immigrants from Hungary. They were deeply devout Christians. They came to this country with no money, no education, and with little family support as only a few distant relatives resided here. As the eldest daughter, I was responsible for taking care of my sister. This became a full time job as we grew older. If there was an issue at Mia's school, I would have to go and speak with the teachers as my parents were always working and they had little command of the English language. I helped her with her homework, coordinated her activities, took her to the doctor and dentist, and acted as a parent. If she needed something, she came to me. I even gave her spending money from my earnings from my jobs after school. My parents made barely enough money to cover our food and shelter.

I was a responsible and dutiful child. I knew that I had to get good grades, and did. I applied to colleges without my parents help, and enrolled in a state school where the tuition was reasonable. I obtained scholarships and took out my own student loans. I then went on to get an MBA which I self funded. My sister, on the other hand, was not able to focus, had more difficulties getting along with people and with doing well in school, and rebelled against our parents' old world ways. She lived for drama, and for agitating people and events. She liked to get a rise out of people, and to see them squirm. She enjoyed that power.

When I was working toward my MBA and living in a one bedroom apartment, Mia moved in with me for about a year because she did not want to live with my parents. I found her extremely difficult to cohabit with. She woke up late, stayed up late, was messy, and had frequent temper tantrums. Her emotional lability was a constant source of stress for me.

She brought home counterculture friends at all hours of the day and night. They would eat all of my food, drink my alcohol, and smoke cigarettes and marijuana. Mia and her friends never paid for anything, and expected me to continually host them. They made fun of my work ethic and work clothes. Mia had odd jobs, but never had a steady income, and always depended upon me to pay for much of her expenses.

She collected people who were continually in crisis, and took them on as personal missions. Her friends were frequently in trouble too. She was always trying to enlist my help with her acquaintances and friends alike. I was often concerned that I would end up on the wrong side of the law by becoming involved. They had a wide range of issues, for instance, arrests for criminal offenses including terrorism or offenses against law enforcement, mental illness, drug and alcohol addiction, unwanted pregnancies, and terminal illnesses and assisted suicide. After a year, I finally told her that she needed to find someplace else to live. She thrived on dysfunction, and I needed discipline, structure, and a quiet life.

Mia moved in with her boyfriend, Kurt, a musician. He, too, never had a steady income. He cheated on her with her friends, but she loved him anyway. He went to prostitutes, but she took him back. He was constantly threatening to commit suicide, and she would, nonetheless, stay by his side when she was not threatening to leave him. I would cook her a meal once a week and bring it to their apartment in order to check up on her. She gave birth to a son, which solidified an already damaged relationship with Kurt. Kurt loved their son, and it helped him to have more meaning in his life. Mia, who had the primary responsibility for their child, loved their son too, but ended up resenting all the time she had to spend on domestic tasks, as she was a free spirit and did not want to be tied down. Mia and Kurt started several businesses together, which failed. They were always in crisis mode.

I married a man named Bob after I had moved to another state where there was more opportunity for my company. My sister Mia did not come to the wedding. She made an excuse, but I knew that deep down she could not accept that I had chosen to live my life with someone. Even though she lived with Kurt, he was not dependable financially or emotionally. He had an unstable childhood as his parents were divorced, his father was mentally ill, and his mother was an alcoholic. Kurt was never able to get over it. And so, my sister's well-being was still on my shoulders. Mia was afraid that I would stop taking care of her once I had my own family.

In addition, Mia deeply resented that I had moved to another state. She felt that I had abandoned her, and our parents, and that she had to take care of our parents, who were ailing, alone. Our parents did not accept Kurt because they did not feel he was hard working and stable enough, and he was not a practicing Christian. They also knew how difficult Mia was, and did not think that anyone else could put up with her behavior, so they tolerated him. Their child, however, brought our parents joy, and they were doting grandparents.

While I sent money to our parents every month, and to my sister for her and her child, Mia insisted, continually, that she did not want to be left behind with responsibility for our parents. I visited as much as I could, but I determined that it was time for me to live my life the way I wanted to. My family would continuously call me and make me feel guilty if I did not do everything they wanted me to do, when they wanted me to do it. While I left physically, they kept a stranglehold on my emotions. Mia was the biggest guilt giver. Her dependency on me felt pathological at times.

My husband was an international tax lawyer with a busy, thriving practice in a large firm. He was not the love of my life, nor I, his. Frankly, it was more a marriage of convenience. We met at a mutual friend's wedding. We had both reached a certain age when our friends were married. We did not have time to date because our work was all encompassing. Since we seemed to be compatible on a number of levels, we decided that it was better than being alone. My husband and I were so busy with our respective careers, we did not try to start a family. By the time we wanted to, I was not able to get pregnant. We were leading independent, parallel lives to a large degree. The inability to create a child together drove us even further apart. Neither of us wanted to adopt as we were afraid to take a chance that our child would not be 'perfect.'

My husband continually criticized and belittled me. If anything went wrong with our finances, with our house, with our car, with our travel, with any arrangements whatsoever, it was my fault. He always wanted me to take care of everything, but when I did, according to him, I never accomplished the tasks correctly. He told me that his friends did not like me because I was outspoken and always said the wrong things. He did not like the foods I ate, and accused me of being too fat. Even though I was making more money than my husband for most of our marriage because of the success of my company, he always mentioned his family's trust fund and how I benefited from his having a wealthy family. He criticized my parents and sister for being 'failures.'

While I was married, my mother and father both died. My husband did not come to either funeral because he was overseas on important business making deals. I developed breast cancer during the latter part of my marriage. He did not accompany me to any of the treatments, and was unsympathetic and impatient when I was tired and my hair fell out from the radiation and chemotherapy treatments. Since we had grown so far apart, I decided I had to leave him.

When I told Mia that my marriage was over, she was thrilled. While I was married, she did everything possible to sabotage my relationship with Bob. When she came to visit with her husband, she would deliberately misbehave. She was rude to Bob, insulted us about our politics, values, home and lifestyle, told me he was boring and not good enough for me, and did everything possible to cause trouble.

On occasion we all took trips together. We had to pay for Mia and her family because they were constantly in and out of jobs. Although we did not mind doing so, she acted as though she were entitled to it. Bob reached the point that he no longer wanted to take trips with Mia because of her bad behavior. Frankly, I did not want to be with her much either. She had an opinion for everything, and always thought she knew best. When she was feeling as though it was time for her to assert her 'power,' she would deliberately do the opposite of something Bob or I requested. If we said not to invite certain friends of hers for a dinner party, she would be certain to invite them and to sit them next to us. One time she invited an old boyfriend of mine to our dinner together just to spite Bob. It made Bob terribly uncomfortable, and I felt protective of him."

I asked Olivia why she thought Mia behaved that way. She said:

"Mia would test my love for her by pitting herself against my spouse to see whom I would sympathize with. There were many versions of that game. She had triangulation down to a science. The sad thing was that her manipulations were readily transparent, and that she could not seem to control herself. In those moments, I did not feel loved by her as it was not loving behavior.

But what was worse was Mia's need for constant attention and nurturing from me, as if I were her parent, and she was still a young child. If we had to spend time with Bob's family, she would accuse me of deserting her and our family. She would insist that we had to spend time together for all kinds of holidays. If I was not able to do what she wanted, about anything, she started to cry. That made me angry and sad at the same time.

Bob had nieces and nephews. Mia resented when we gave them gifts and attention, and said they were not my family, only her son was. She knew that I had a good heart and was protective of her. But, in trying to remain the most important person in my life, she continually manipulated me by talking badly about the other people in my world whom I loved.

For a time, after my divorce, Mia was in all her glory. We went to spas together, took vacations, and had most holidays together. She had me to herself. When Bob's family no longer paid attention to me, and stopped communicating with me, because they took his side in the divorce, Mia insisted that she could have predicted that behavior all along, and that they were not my family. She told me what a sucker I was to have lavished all that time, attention and money on them with no return."

I asked Olivia how she felt when Mia said those things. She said:

"I felt suffocated by Mia's dependencies on me. I wanted her to focus on her own husband and child. Her marriage was always in turmoil, and yet she did not want to leave him and said she still loved him. She could not live with him, and she could not live without him. Because of that, it seemed that she could not wean herself from me. She went to a therapist, but it did not seem to help in that regard."

I asked her if she discussed these feelings with Mia. She said:

"I did not have the heart to tell her because I felt sorry for her. But then my feelings of sympathy became mixed with a renewed sense of anger. The trouble with Mia's insecurities and jealousy began again, full blast, once I started a new relationship.

After my divorce, I had been dating for a few years, but I wanted to meet someone to settle down with. I finally met Tibor when I was in my forties through an upscale dating service. Tibor was an engineer. Tibor's wife had died, and he had an adult son and adult daughter. His son, Brian, was a doctor. His daughter, Kaitlin, was a graphic designer. They were both married, and each had one child. They were a fully functional family. They were all stable, hard working, and independent. The adults had a good education and accomplished careers, and their children were being raised in loving homes in safe communities.

From the moment Tibor and I met, we had a deep connection. We could talk easily for hours without boring one another. We were attracted to one another physically. We were intellectually compatible, and shared similar interests including the arts, music, science and technology. His family was originally from Hungary, so we had ethnicity in common. We were both practicing Christians, and liberals politically. After our first date, we spent all of our free time together. His friends accepted me, and my friends accepted him. Our circle was getting wider and richer.

After six months, we decided that since we were not getting any younger, he would move into my apartment so that we could spend more time together as our professional lives were busy. Tibor's children were thrilled that we found each other and that we were a loving couple. They loved their father, and worried that he was lonely since their mother died. They welcomed me into their family, and made me feel loved in a way I had never known before. All of a sudden, I became both a pseudo parent and grandparent for the first time. Brian and Kaitlin said that I should consider myself a real family member and grandparent. Their children called me Nana.

In contrast, when I contacted my sister to tell her the good news about Tibor and I living together, she started berating me for not telling her before we did so. She told me that I knew how marriage had worked out for me, and that this would not end well, just as my marriage to Bob did not. Tibor and I emailed her a video of the two of us dancing happily in our apartment, which we had re-decorated by incorporating Tibor's possessions, and she never returned an email. She never truly wished us well by e-mail or by telephone. She told me that Tibor was not my husband and that Brian and Kaitlin's children were not my grandchildren. She told me that I did not pay enough attention to her son, and that I was the most important person in her son's life. She told me that he needed a new computer, and that I should buy one for his birthday.

Tibor and I met Mia for dinner one time soon after we had moved in together. She never brought her husband to see me because he never wanted to come. Or, maybe, Mia just wanted me to herself. When I went to the bathroom, she told Tibor that my relationship with him would never last as she knew me, and she gave it two years at most. Tibor was shocked by these words of cruelty, and told me about it later when we were alone.

Mia was up to her triangulation tricks once again. She wanted Tibor to know that she was the one constant in my life, and that he would not be. Now she had succeeded in alienating Tibor, just as she had alienated Bob. And, what was particularly distressing, is that she delighted in putting me in the middle to test my love and devotion to her. I knew this behavior was the product of a sick mind. Again, I felt sorry for her that her own life was so unhappy that she would have to resort to trying to make me miserable along with her."

I asked Olivia if she confronted Mia about this. She said:

"My sister and I have trouble addressing issues between us directly. She always ends up crying, and then I feel guilty. Usually she just denies that she said or did anything wrong. She turns it around on me, and says that I failed to do something correctly which caused the problem. In this case, she denied that she said that to Tibor, but then said she thought that it was true, that I would leave him.

She had another tactic she used to cause trouble. After I finally confronted her and asked her why she attacked the people closest to me, instead of responding, she invoked the memories of our parents as she knows that it will make me feel guilty. She insisted that we celebrate their birthdays, their anniversary, or some other marker now that they are deceased. If I could not do it for scheduling reasons, she accused me of preferring my new family, and of leaving her and her family behind. She turned it into a competition, and would not let me love other people freely. I resented her terribly for that, as I did not feel that it came from a place of love."

I asked Olivia if she thought her sister loved her. She said:

"I do think that she loves me on one level. But on another level, if she really loved me, she would be happy that Tibor and his family love me also, and that I have finally found happiness after my difficult divorce. She knows that I had wanted to have my own children. She should be happy for me that Tibor's children have made me feel as though I were an additional parent, and most assuredly, another grandparent to their children. Love should not be given possessively and with conditions, the way she does."

Mia continued to try to make trouble for Olivia at every turn. Olivia was grateful that she lived far enough away from Mia that she did not have to deal with her physically on a regular basis. Tibor understood Mia's issues and tried to support Olivia emotionally. By identifying the issues, and by learning to confront Mia more directly, Olivia was able to feel less guilty over time. She eventually recognized that these were Mia's issues and not her own, and that she had done everything she could do to be a loving sister. There was no fixing Mia unless Mia wanted to be fixed with her own therapist. Olivia continued to maintain a relationship with Mia, but on new and healthier terms.

Olivia became better about creating appropriate boundaries between herself and her sister. She realized that she had a right to be happy, and that nobody could or should try to take that away from her. She also came to accept that she no longer wanted to have a parental role with Mia, and that she did not want Mia trying to tell her how to live her life. She forgave Mia for her weaknesses and faults, but she made certain that Mia could no longer hurt her, or the people she loved, anymore.

Chapter Eleven

Body Image and Weight

"When you believe in yourself more than you believe in food, you will stop using food as if it were your only chance at not falling apart."

Geneen Roth

"The hardest challenge is to be yourself in a world where everyone is trying to make you be someone else."

E.E. Cummings

A young woman named Esme began treatment with me when she was in her early thirties. She was married, and worked in a responsible job in government as an accountant. She did not have to interact with many people at work, as she crunched numbers for much of the day. She was morbidly obese. She was unable to get pregnant because of her weight, and she had become increasingly depressed. She hated herself for being fat, and now she had another reason to punish herself. Her fat was preventing her from having a child.

Notwithstanding how Esme felt inside, she had an upbeat personality. She smiled frequently and made intelligent, insightful, funny remarks. She wore black tent dresses in an attempt to hide the weight, bright colored scarves, and flat shoes. She always had her hair in an attractive style, with a full face of carefully applied makeup, and painted fingernails. Everything about her indicated that she was someone who paid attention to her appearance, and took care of herself, except for her weight.

Esme had been obese her entire life. Both of her parents, and her brother, were obese as well. She was born in the United States. Her family was originally from Mexico, and her parents had been citizens in the United States for many years.

I asked her about what her early years were like. She said:

"I experienced discrimination from other families and from teachers because of my ethnicity, although that was the least of it. From the time I was a little girl, I was significantly overweight. We did not have much money then, and for a treat, if we went out, we ate a lot of junk food from McDonalds and other fast food restaurants. When we cooked food at home, we ate large quantities of rice and beans and sweets. If I cried, my parents gave me food. If I was happy and we had something to celebrate, my parents gave me food. If I was frustrated doing my homework, my parents gave me food. If I was bored and they wanted to keep me quiet, they gave me food. Whenever I felt any emotions, food was offered as love to make me feel better. We had a large, extended family with many family events. Food was always the main attraction for me at those parties. In fact, my entire life revolved around food from an early age.

I learned to reward myself with food over time. I was a latchkey child because my parents both worked at a deli business they eventually owned. I came home from school with my little brother, and we ate whatever we wanted to from the refrigerator and cabinets until my parents arrived. Nobody told us what we could and could not eat. Sometimes we ate an entire box of cookies before dinner. Then my parents would either cook, or bring home some food from the deli for dinner.

Nobody in my family liked to move around much. We preferred sedentary activities. Our favorite activity for relaxation was to sit in front of the television set, watch our favorite shows or movies, and eat treats. If we went out, we preferred going to the movies over a walk. My parents had significant health problems because of their weight, but they continued working. We rarely talked about their weight, or mine, until I was in high school."

I asked her if being overweight was a problem for her at school. She told me:

"I was teased terribly at school. I was bullied from the time I was five-years-old. On the schoolbus, the children would taunt me and call me names such as cow, pig, lazy, and ugly. They would imitate how I walked with a waddle. Nobody wanted to sit with me at lunch as early as elementary school. Sometimes the boys would throw food at me in the cafeteria. The girls would look me up and down and snicker amongst themselves. Some children made pig noises when they saw me. I was called fat on a daily basis, and sometimes they would say that my entire family was fat. I watched my brother being bullied too.

Some of the children became physically aggressive with me. For instance, at recess, they pushed me down on the ground, and then ground my face in the dirt and told me to eat the dirt. I was excluded from being chosen on school athletic teams because nobody wanted the slow, fat girl. I was not invited to the sleepover parties with the other girls, or to their birthday parties or after school events.

I had one close friend at school, Catalina, in elementary, middle and high school. She was from a family with South American heritage, and was overweight too. If not for her, I would not have made it through. Because my social life was limited from an early age, I spent a lot of time reading and doing homework, so the teachers generally liked me and gave me good grades. Catalina was also a good student. It was more difficult for her at home because her family was not overweight, and her mother abused her about her weight on a daily basis. Catalina's self esteem was even worse than mine, if that is possible."

I asked Esme if she ever told anyone about the bullying at school. She said:

"I did not grow up at a time when they had as much education about bullying as they do now. I knew that if I told on any of the other children, my life would have been even more difficult. I was already considered a teacher's pet and despised because of that. It was not 'cool' to be a good student in the schools I attended. If I became responsible for getting those students in trouble, that would have elevated the abuse toward me to a new level. For the most part I swallowed my feelings, literally and figuratively. When the other students teased me, I ate even more. My parents always gave me spending money. After a bullying incident, I stopped off, routinely, at Dunkin Donuts on the way home from school, and ate an entire box of donuts at home, in one sitting, with my brother."

I asked Esme how she felt after she ate a lot of food. She said:

"Food became my comfort, and my anguish. While I initially felt better when I had something sweet or salty in my mouth, because I kept eating past the point of comfort, I had terrible digestion problems. I felt even worse about myself after a binge. I hated looking in the mirror, and rarely did. I cannot remember a single day when I liked my body. My rolls of fat on my belly, legs, and back, in particular, disgusted me. I was constantly trying to devise a way to hide the fat as much as possible.

I had problems finding fashionable clothes that fit. My weight fluctuated so that I never had enough to wear. The only time I had to truly face how much I had gained was when I dressed and clothes no longer fit. I knew that I was addicted to food, but could not stop myself. It did not help that my parents were fat and in the food business at their deli. Their lives revolved around food too. Everywhere I turned, while watching television, reading magazines, looking at subway ads, or walking in the street, there were advertisements for food. The portion sizes served everywhere, from the diner, to my parents home, were too large. There were many factors conspiring against my ability to maintain a healthy weight.

When I was in high school, I tried many diets. While I was on them, I would lose some weight, and people would tell me I looked better, which only made me feel worse about my weight. But it was torture for me to be on them, and once I stopped the diet, I quickly gained back the weight I lost, and more. The problem with a food addiction is that you still have to eat every day, and controlling what you eat and how much is so challenging for an addict. My mother took me to a doctor because I complained to her about how unhappy I was about my weight. The doctor told me that I had a slow metabolism, and a genetic predisposition to being overweight. He told me to eat less and to exercise more. He gave me pamphlets about healthy foods to eat, and in what proportion to eat them, and books on exercise and burning calories. I needed the education, but I also knew in my heart that knowing what was correct to do was not going to be enough for me. There was an emotional component that had to be dealt with."

We talked about how her weight impacted her dating in high school and after. She said:

"When I was in high school, no one wanted to date me. I was a social pariah. Going out with me would mean losing many points on the social hierarchy scale. I was not invited to any of the socials or to prom. I was essentially an outcast because of my weight. Some of the 'nicer' boys would say that I was too heavy, and that they would go out with me if I was not so fat. I received the message that I was unlovable, and was not a sexual being. No one would ever consider having sex with someone as fat as me.

One day after school I was walking home alone. Four boys from school attacked me and pulled me into an alley. They made horrible animal noises, told me that I smelled like a barn, and started to try to pull my clothes off. They pushed me onto the ground and one of the boys jumped on top of me, while the other boys laughed. At that moment, a few people walked into the alley, and the boys ran away. My clothes were torn and I was shaking. I would not have been able to fight off four boys. I never told anyone what happened because I was so ashamed. I saw the boys at school, and they would just wink at me and make noises, but they did not try to touch me again. I started to carry a rape whistle with me after that, and tried not to walk alone. That incident made me feel even more ashamed about my body, and made me hate it even more.

There were many other moments of humiliation for me in high school with some being more serious than others. In health class we had a segment on obesity. The teacher talked about how obesity in childhood can result in health problems, often for life. She talked about how in adults, it is linked to an increased risk of heart disease, type 2 diabetes, high blood pressure, certain cancers, and other chronic conditions. She told us that the data suggested that overweight and obesity are having a greater effect on minorities, including Blacks and Hispanics. Everybody turned to me, and a few of the boys made barnyard sounds. I was obese and Hispanic. I was afraid that my teacher was going to call me to the head of the class to show all the students a real life example of what she was talking about, an honor and distinction I did not want. I was certain that after that lecture, I was not going to be asked out on a date, ever.

While I was in college, I met my future husband in an accounting class. He was the first and only boy I ever dated. He, too, was overweight, and he did not hold my weight against me. He was of Puerto Rican descent, although also born in the United States. We had similar backgrounds and experiences. We were from hard working immigrant families who had their own businesses; we did well in school; we had no social lives before we met each other; and we had been bullied and teased about our respective weight for our entire lives.

We both became certified public accountants, obtained jobs in New York City, married, and bought a small house on Staten Island. We have remained obese."

We talked about why she continued to have weight issues. She said:

"I never dreamed that I would meet a man I loved, that I would get married, and that I would have a good job. All of that came true for me, but I have not lost weight. My parents both died of heart attacks shortly after I married, which was not surprising given their obesity. We were close, and my grief was intense. I ate my feelings when all of that happened. Then my husband developed prostate cancer, which was highly unusual to get at his age, and I went through the stress of that with him. I worried about his health and our bills. We made it through that scare, but as always, I used food as a crutch and comfort to get me through difficult times.

I had pressure at work with deadlines and a difficult boss. Sometimes when the pressure mounted, I bought a large bag of candy and went into the bathroom and ate it to calm myself down. While it calmed me momentarily, the sugar wreaked havoc on my mood stability. Then I felt down about myself and the self-hatred continued unabated.

Being obese held me back at work. I have not received the promotions I should have. I have not made as much money as thinner women and men have. I was never given a position with much contact with people as my bosses thought that my size would make me less effective. Because I worked in government, the pay disparity was not as great, but I have definitely been hurt by my size.

In addition to the discrimination in title, position, and pay, my co-workers have been unkind to me at work. When I ate lunch in the conference room, they watched what I ate and made negative comments about the food and the quantity. They talked about working out in the gym, and other physical activities outside, and told me that I should do that. If I took off days for illness, my boss and co-workers said that if I lost weight I would not get sick as much. When women talked about work clothes, they looked at me and said that those clothes did not come in my size. They talked about how obesity is a drain on the economy, and that people who are fat are lazy and have no discipline. I ate my lunch at my desk most days because I found all of the comments hurtful and insensitive.

But the problems did not end at the office door. When I took public transportation, boarded a plane, went to a movie theatre, attended a concert, or went to a supermarket, people gave me dirty looks because I took up so much space. Even though I have a loving husband, my experience outside the home remained humiliating and painful.

When it came to food at home, my husband and I have been bad influences on each other. He loved to cook, and encouraged me to eat his latest creations, which were always high in calories. We enjoyed quiet activities like reading and listening to music, so we don't get the exercise we should. We are both so tired after work, we just want to park ourselves in front of the television and relax."

We talked about her sex life with her husband. She told me:

"My husband was the first person I ever had sex with. I was self conscious about my body in front of everybody, including him. I never went swimming or to the beach because I did not want to be seen in a bathing suit. I think he understood that about me. When we had sex, I made sure I was either in bed with the covers over me before he came into the room, or I wrapped myself in a towel from the bathroom and took it off after I was under the covers. I made sure that the lights were off when we had sex, and still do. Unlike me, he was not self- conscious about his body, which helped me to feel more comfortable.

It was difficult for me to have positive feelings about my body. My body image was completely destroyed with all the bullying and abuse I have taken over the years. That interfered with my enjoyment of sex. I always worried about whether my fat was hanging over when I turned in different directions while we were having sex. I did not prefer my husband to touch the meatier portions of me. I did not tell him that I was not having orgasms because he was pleasured, so I did not want to take that away from him.

Over time, and with my husband's love and acceptance, I have been able to relax more than I did initially. I still have remnants of those old feelings, but he always told me that I was beautiful and I believed that he thought that. I do not know if I will ever feel completely at home in my body. Believe it or not I have never masturbated much as I have been that uncomfortable in my own skin. It may be that I don't think that I have as much of a right to pleasure as other people do. I never wanted to draw my own attention to my own body. I always told myself that if I lost weight and was able to keep it off, that I would love myself more, and that my confidence would improve."

We talked about Esme wanting a child. I asked her about her feelings about that. She said:

"In my culture, and for me personally, having a child is the most important thing a woman can do. I was raised to revere children, and to view having them as an essential role for me. My husband was raised in a similar culture. We had frequent sex in the hope that I would get pregnant. We tried for two years without success.

We finally went to a fertility specialist. We learned that my obesity was making it difficult for me to get pregnant. We learned that my husband's obesity and his bout with prostate cancer had impacted on his sperm count. Now, once again, we felt that we had only ourselves to blame. We joined a gym, but we did not lose weight because the exercise made us hungry, and we ate too much when we went home. We could not keep to a diet.

We both considered having bariatric surgery. We learned about gastric bypass surgery as one of the most common types of bariatric surgery. We were told that even that procedure could pose serious risks and side effects, such as 'excessive bleeding, infection, adverse reactions to anesthesia, blood clots, lung or breathing problems leaks in our gastrointestinal system, and even, but rarely, death.'

We were told that some long term risks and complications of weight loss surgery can include 'bowel obstruction, dumping syndrome, gallstones, hernias, low blood sugar, malnutrition, stomach perforation, ulcers, vomiting, and even, but rarely, death.' We also learned that the surgery may not work, and we could gain the weight back. In fact, my husband had a cousin who gained the weight back after surgery and suffered from many complications.

We were told that we needed to wait for maximum weight loss before I tried to get pregnant. We were told that having the surgery and losing the weight usually improved the ability to get pregnant.

My husband and I had a lot of stress even thinking about all of the options. It created tension between us. We wanted to lose the weight for our self-esteem. We wanted to lose the weight so that we could have children together. But I was terrified of the surgery and convinced that I would keep eating and gain back the weight. I was concerned about the expense of the surgeries. He wanted us to have the surgery as he was more optimistic than I. He believed that it was an important investment in our future so that we could have children and get healthier ourselves. He viewed it as a win-win. I started to feel increasingly pressured, and gained weight from 'eating my feelings' once again."

Over many months, I worked with Esme so that she could better understand how her weight problem started, what contributed to it remaining an issue, and strategies to use when she felt like bingeing. She joined an overeaters support group. We worked on her confidence issues, and her depression.

She had not decided whether she will have the bariatric surgery as of our latest session. She put the decision on hold for six months while she worked through her issues. She had many positives in her favor including a loving husband, high intelligence, a strong work ethic, a good career, and a psychological support network. Most of all, she had a loving heart which will help her to make decisions that make sense. My hope for her is that she will allow her heart to love herself, fat or thin.

Chapter Twelve

Senior Seeking Peace: Elder Suicide

*"How incessant and great are the ills with which
a prolonged old age is replete."*

C.S. Lewis

"This above all, to thine own self be true."

Shakespeare

Marilyn was an eighty-five-year-old woman who first came into treatment for chronic depression, which I treated with antidepressants. Despite the fact that she described how excruciating life had become for her on a physical basis, she came to each session at my office impeccably dressed, with a youthful exuberance and enthusiasm in her voice, and a grace and charm she clearly had for her entire life. Physically, she was a shrunken version of herself. She was painfully thin, with spindly legs that could barely hold up her meager weight. She first used a cane, later a walker, and then a wheelchair, before her life ended.

At her first session, she told me that she wanted to die, and that so did all of her close friends. According to Marilyn, they all believed that they had lived too long, and that their physical infirmities had robbed them of their dignity, and their ability to enjoy their lives. I asked her when her physical pain first started. She said:

"When I was in my late fifties, I was happily married with two adult daughters. My husband Hugh and I lived in Manhattan. We had a summer house which we rented in Maine. One Friday night, my husband was exhausted from work, but insisted on driving to our house, which was approximately six hours away. He was a financial analyst, and had a particularly rough week. He needed to escape. I worked as a special education teacher at the time. I did not experience my work as stressful, but rather as a gift. I agreed that we should go. I tried to make his life calmer, and I knew when he needed an outlet. I quickly packed, we retrieved the car from our parking garage, and went on our way.

Hugh preferred to do all of the driving. It made him too nervous when I drove, as I tended to drive at or below the speed limit, and would not even attempt to get around slow moving vehicles, which made him impatient. He wanted to get everywhere quickly and efficiently. I liked to meander and take my time. That example describes our basic temperaments. I imagine we were a good couple because of our different, but complementary, personality traits.

After about three hours of driving, we stopped at a gas station and I bought him some coffee. I decided to get some sleep in the back seat. I curled up with a blanket over me, listened to some classical music which Hugh played on the radio, and drifted off. It was a time when the use of seatbelts was emphasized less. Some time later, I heard a terrible crashing sound, I smelled smoke, and I was propelled against the back of the front seat. I do not remember much after that. Apparently, I was taken from the vehicle on a stretcher to an ambulance and driven to a nearby hospital. I never saw Hugh again as I was told that he died at the scene.

My daughters came to the hospital the next day. We were all in shock. They were and are a great comfort to me. After x-rays and a CT scan, I was told that I had spinal fractures, and a fracture of my neck. I had severe pain at the site of the fractures, and in my arms and legs. I needed to wear braces for twelve weeks, and had six weeks of physical therapy. I did not have surgery.

While I was still in terrible physical pain, I planned my husband's funeral. Later, I had to move to a smaller apartment. I was unable to return to work as a special education teacher because of my physical infirmities, so I retired. I grieved Hugh's death for a long time. I was physically never the same, but I did recover.

In addition to my grief and my physical issues, I had financial pressures. Unfortunately, Hugh had not kept up the payments for his life insurance, so I did not benefit from that. I also learned that he had incurred some debt which I did not know about, which had to be paid off from his estate. He handled all of the finances for our entire marriage. I had to educate myself to become financially savvy and independent, which was a huge learning curve. Eventually I realized that with my teacher's pension from thirty plus years of teaching, my relatively inexpensive health care, and with the money saved from moving to a smaller apartment, I could survive, although not nearly at the same lifestyle level that I had enjoyed previously. I did not want my daughters to have to take care of me in any way, although they were both well educated, had careers, and told me to never worry about money. I knew that many women were not nearly as fortunate as I, but it did take an adjustment when my financial status declined."

I asked Marilyn if she had psychological therapy then. She said:

"I was not a person prone to depression. Even after going through those difficult life events, I was able to remain hopeful, and to turn my life around in a more positive direction on my own. I did not go to individual therapy. I was so busy with my physical therapy, and with the pain management clinic, that I did not address anything else then. I had my daughters, and some good, old friends, who supported me during that period. My mother was alive at that time, and she was an enormous psychological support as well. I joined a book club and took courses in subjects I had always been interested in, but never had the time to pursue. I started a small business selling wedding invitations. I was active in my Church.

Although I kept busy, I missed my husband and male companionship. I did not think that at my age I would ever meet anybody again. Nonetheless, three years after Hugh's death, I met a man, Jack, through mutual friends. He was seven years my senior, and in good health. His wife had died of brain cancer. He had taken care of her through all of her medical issues, for many years. He was a nurturer by nature, and I felt that I needed someone like that. He had dated many women after his wife died, and by the time I met him, he seemed to want to settle down. We fell in love, and after five years, we married. He loved to travel, and despite my physical limitations, I went everywhere with him. He loved to cook, and did all of it. We enjoyed theatre, lectures, museums, and all the cultural events New York City had to offer. He liked to control things, and I did not mind since he doted on me. I knew how lucky I was to find him, and he enjoyed my company.

Jack had one son, Bob. Bob was a Professor and he was married to a successful businesswoman. They never had children. They had an apartment in Manhattan and a house in Greece. Bob had been particularly close to his mother when she was alive. Bob's mother had been a Professor, had written many prize winning books, and was highly intellectual. I was not nearly as ambitious, although I had a long and rewarding career.

From the time that I first started to date Jack, Bob did not want to accept me into the family. He told Jack that he was concerned that I would take all of Jack's money, and that there would be little left for Bob to inherit. He did not like that I had a bad back, neck and physical limitations. He told his father that he would end up taking care of me for the rest of my life, and that Jack did not need that after having taken care of Bob's mother all of those years. Bob did not respect how I spent my time, or what I had achieved in my life. Bob made it apparent that in his view, his father had chosen a lesser person than his mother.

Bob's lack of love and acceptance of me hurt Jack deeply, as it did me. The few times we all were together each year, Bob continually spoke of his mother in my presence. Bob made it clear that I could never take the place of his mother in any way. Our relationship never evolved from being highly uncomfortable, into something else which was more accepting. Jack loved Bob and his wife, and he loved me. He did not like to feel that he had to choose. Eventually, Jack started to meet Bob on his own for lunch, and that took the pressure off of everybody.

Jack had become close to my daughters, their husbands, and their children, over time. Since Bob did not have children of his own, he resented his father for taking vacations with my daughters and their families. Initially, I invited Bob and his wife to our family gatherings, but they either made excuses that they could not come because the date was not good for them even if given notice many months in advance, or if they were given a week or two notice, they said that we needed to give them more notice. If they did attend, they would show up late or leave early, they tended to drink too much, and kept to themselves. They did not want to be there. Bob made me feel as if we had kidnapped his father from him. They rarely invited Jack and I to their apartment in New York or to their home in Greece, and they rarely came to our apartment. When we all met, it was at a restaurant. Sometimes blended families cannot blend. Jack and I made our peace with that.

Although Jack got along well with my daughters for the most part, my elder daughter thought that he was too bossy and that he controlled me too much. She felt that I was a refined and classy person, and that Jack was blunt and heavy handed. He also liked to drink and eat a lot which my daughters did not approve of. At family events, sometimes he would get sloppy drunk and would flirt with the young women. Their father had been slim and disciplined about food and exercise and he did not drink. He did not overtly flirt that way either. These were not Jack's traits that I enjoyed, particularly, but he was good to me, and I reasoned that everyone has to put up with something. For the most part, he was fun, lively, energetic, entertaining and interesting. As a companion in my elder years, that was a good formula for me. I did not have to raise children with him, and my daughters were grown and able to deal with his relatively minor indiscretions. He took an interest in my family, and seemed to love and care about them."

I asked Marilyn what made her come to see me for therapy. She said:

"When I reached my eighties, the pain in my back and neck became intolerable. I was taking heavy medication just to get through the day. I was going to a pain clinic to learn how to manage the pain, to no avail. I had seen many surgeons about having back surgery, but when they told me the risks and the likelihood of success, I did not want to do it. I had scheduled surgery several times, and cancelled it each time.

I had always been someone with high energy. At that point in my life, if I went out during the day, I had to rest in the evening, and if I went out in the evening, I had to rest during the day. It became more and more difficult for me to move. Jack had to do everything for me. He hired a housekeeper to clean, and he did all of the food shopping and cooking. I cancelled plans with my friends on a frequent basis because I was in too much pain to get out of bed. Jack sometimes became impatient with me, and I felt guilty if he cancelled plans in order to stay home with me. It put a strain on our relationship, but he remained devoted.

My physical condition continued to decline at a rapid rate. Increasingly, I felt that I should see a therapist to fully explore my decision to commit suicide, and that is when I made an appointment to see you."

After six months in therapy, I asked Marilyn if she still thought about committing suicide. She said:

"It has helped me to speak with you. Even though you have given me antidepressants, increased the dosage, and given me some relief, I remain convinced that my life is not worth living anymore. I do not think that depression is driving the decision. I believe that sometimes people live too long, and that they should be able to die with dignity.

I have researched, on the internet, ways in which to commit suicide. I could never put a bag over my head and inhale helium, shoot myself, starve myself, hang myself or jump off a building or bridge. As you know, it is not illegal to commit suicide, but it is illegal for someone to assist you with it. The only suicide method which appealed to me was to take liquid pentobarbital, which is sold under the trade name Nembutal. As you know, it is a fast acting barbiturate used by veterinarians to euthanize domestic and farm animals. I could mix it with limeade powder and sugar as the taste would be too bitter. It is difficult to get Nembutal in this Country. I understand that it is available in Mexico.

Also, I want to be assisted in my suicide, preferably by a physician, so that there is no chance that I could throw up the medicine and botch it, and I could be certain to take the appropriate dosage. I am not a resident of any State which allows assisted suicide legally, and my condition would not be considered terminal, so I probably would not be eligible in those States even if I lived there. My best chance to do it in a way which is palatable to me is to go to Switzerland and arrange for it there. They do not have a residency requirement It is very expensive, but worth it to me."

It made me sad to hear Marilyn speak that way, and I felt torn as a therapist because on some level I felt I had failed. I tried not to judge her decision in any way, but to understand it. I asked Marilyn if her husband and daughters approved of her decision. She said:

"My daughters do not want me to do it, but they understand that everybody should be able to die with dignity, and that my life had become too painful. They agreed to be at my bedside in Switzerland before and after the infusion of medication. The only hitch was that it would be incredibly difficult for me to physically fly in a plane for that many hours to get there.

Jack, on the other hand, did not want to let me go. He did not want to live without me. He felt that I should keep fighting this, and not give up. He had a philosophical opposition to suicide. He was a World War II veteran, and has a certain view of the world borne from those experiences. He never had a serious illness, and never experienced chronic and unrelenting pain, so he could not truly understand how intolerable my life had become.

I explained to him that I love him, but that I cannot go on. I cannot do anything for myself anymore. I need assistance to dress, to eat, to shower and to go to the bathroom. I no longer want to eat, but I cannot starve myself. Jack keeps trying to feed me. I am never completely free of pain. I drink alcohol too much with my medication, to escape, and I end up feeling sick all of the time. My mind is starting to deteriorate because of all of the medication I have to take. My short term memory is worse and worse. I have trouble reading a book or watching television. I cannot sit through a movie or a concert, and I cannot attend classes or my book group. I cannot sit in a car, or a bus for any length of time so I cannot visit my children. Managing the subway is impossible. It is so painful to go from my bed into my wheelchair, that I don't want to do it anymore. I do not see my friends anymore unless they come to see me, and most are too infirm to do so.

My life is limited to the four walls of my bedroom and my bed. I only leave the apartment to go to doctor appointments, and those visits have become too much of an ordeal. I do not want to go to a nursing home. I am no longer eligible for an assisted living facility, and Jack and I would not want to live in one. He is in his nineties now, and I do not want to burden him with my care. We do not want a home health care worker in our apartment. We value our privacy, and do not want someone living with us, or even spending the day in our apartment. In our view, our apartment is not large enough for three people.

I have run out of options. I need to leave this world now. I am a humanist. We put animals to sleep to put them out of their misery. Why should we do less for a human being?"

We talked about how her friends felt about her wanting to commit suicide. She said:

"I have discussed this decision with my best girlfriends. They, too, have intolerable disabilities. They have been fighting for their physical and mental health for years. We are all in our late eighties. A few of my girlfriends do not have enough money, so they could not afford to go to Switzerland. I don't even know if I could actually make the trip physically, as I have said, even though money is not a problem for me. A few are too scared to commit suicide by any method, even if a physician assisted it. Most of my friends are religious Christians, and would not dream of doing it for religious reasons. They have tried to talk me out of it, and are afraid I will end up eternally damned, in hell."

I asked her how she felt about the religious aspect of committing suicide. She said:

"I believe in God and I have been a regular Churchgoer for my entire life. I am also an independent thinker. I do not believe that God would want me, or anyone else, to suffer needlessly. I do not believe in a punishing God. I have led a decent, honorable, and law abiding life. I do not have a problem squaring my decision with my religious upbringing. There are doctors who give their patients extra morphine when they are in hospice so that they can die painlessly and peacefully. Even though I do not have a terminal illness, so I am not eligible for hospice, I cannot live with the disability I have.

I am not a political person. I have never become involved in the wave of organizations after the Hemlock Society. I am not involved in the Right to Die movement. I do believe that as the baby boomers reach the stage that I am at in increasing numbers, there will be increased pressure to change the laws in more states to allow for physician assisted suicide, with certain limitations, which would include my situation.

Not all of my friends agree with me. They are concerned that depressed people will use the right improperly, that doctors will misuse it to make money, that families will kill off other family members to get the money in their wills, that teens will misuse it, and on and on. My understanding is that in the few States that allow for it in this Country, such as Oregon, there has not been an increase in the amount of suicides, nor have any of those fears been realized."

As a therapist, I felt conflicted. On the one hand, I was concerned that Marilyn's desire to commit suicide might be part of her depression that even medication could not fully treat. I had a high regard for the sanctity of life. As a religious person, it did not square with my upbringing, or with my religious affiliations. On the other hand, Marilyn had made a decision about how she wanted to live, and how she wanted to die, like one does in a living will. She did not want me or anyone else to resuscitate her, as it were. I had a high regard for a person's dignity, and right to self determination. After all, it was her body, and she had lived a long life. No one was forcing her hand. In fact, many were trying to convince her otherwise.

At our last session, she told me that she would not be coming back to see me. I tried to convince her otherwise, but she was determined. She thanked me for the therapy, and told me that my sensitivity and loving acceptance of her had meant much to her and had helped her to get through a difficult period. She had made her decision to go to Switzerland, and nothing could sway her from that course. We hugged one another and cried. I was an additional person who would miss her.

I asked her if I had permission to contact Jack and her daughters after the trip to Switzerland. She told me that Jack had finally agreed to be by her bedside, along with her daughters. Jack's son, Bob, did not want to be involved. She gave me Jack's contact information, and that of her daughters, and told me that she was happy that I would contact them after her death.

A few months later I tried to contact Jack. I called the answering machine, and Marilyn's voice was still on it. I left several messages, but never heard back from him. I then contacted Marilyn's eldest daughter. She told me that soon after Marilyn terminated the therapy with me, and before she had a chance to go to Switzerland, Marilyn fell in her bedroom, and hit her head on the dresser. Jack called 911 immediately, and an ambulance took her to the hospital, where she went into a coma, and died a few days later from intracranial bleeding in her brain. Jack slept by her side in the hospital, and was there when she died. Her daughters were with her in the hospital room during the hours before she passed.

I learned from Marilyn's daughter, also, that Jack went to visit his son Bob in Greece a few months after Marilyn's death. Jack was grieving terribly, and was talking about taking his own life. He did not want to live without Marilyn. While in Greece, after drinking too much, Jack took a fall down a flight of stairs in Bob's home, and died. It was a Greek tragedy, on so many levels. I hope that Marilyn and Jack are reunited, and that they are no longer in any pain, mentally or physically. They had suffered too much at the end.

Chapter Thirteen

Adoptee Seeking Closure

"Being adopted is like having blank pages in the first chapter of your book of life."

Adult Adoptee

"Adoption carries the added dimension of connection not only to your own tribe but beyond, widening the scope of what constitutes love, ties, and family. It is the larger embrace."

Isabella Rossellini

I met Sarah when she was in her twenties. She came into treatment after she gave birth to her first child. Sarah had been trained as a family therapist, and had sensitivity and awareness beyond her years. She was a strikingly beautiful young woman. She was tall, had dark curly hair, light brown skin, and appeared to be biracial. There was something in her expression which showed that she was struggling in a profound way. She told me that since she gave birth, unresolved issues involving her own past kept surfacing, and she no longer felt she could avoid dealing with them. She wanted to be the best wife and mother she could be.

I asked her about her background. She told me:

"I was adopted when I was an infant by my adoptive parents, Karen and Kenneth, both of whom were doctors. After I was adopted, three years later, Karen was able to get pregnant, and gave birth to my sister, Nicole, who had blonde hair and blue eyes. We did not look like sisters, and we did not appear to be from the same tribe. As we grew up, my interests and skill set were different from my family. I was artistic and excelled in the fine arts and dance. My sister, who was similar to my adoptive parents, was math and science oriented.

My parents told me early on that I had been adopted. They continually reassured me that they loved me and that I was special to them. They never showed favoritism toward my sister, and during the early years, I did not think much about what being adopted meant. I felt a certain pressure to be a 'good girl' so that my parents would never make me leave. There was an underlying anxiety about abandonment, even if it had not risen to the surface. I felt protective of my sister, and she of me. We were always close, and nobody in the family ever made me feel 'lesser than.'

The schools we went to did not have many students who looked like me. They were predominantly white. On occasion the other children would ask why my sister and I looked so different, and why I did not look like my parents. They would ask me who my real parents were, and what happened to them. I thought of my adoptive parents as my real parents, so the questions confused me. Then, I would go home and ask my parents to explain it to me.

Karen told me that she did not have much information about my birth mother. It was a closed adoption. All that Karen learned was that she was a teenage mother, and that she was not equipped to raise me so that she had to put me up for adoption. Karen did not know anything about my birth father. That level of information satisfied me for a long time, but I felt ashamed to share that information with friends.

Also, I sensed from my parents that they did not want to talk much about the adoption. I felt as though I was being disloyal to them when I tried to. I denied to myself that I needed to know more, and shoved my feelings down. I expressed to them how grateful I was for what they did for me, which made me feel like an 'other.'

I lived a comfortable life in a safe suburb of Chicago. My education was superior, and I had everything I needed materially, and more. My feelings of discontent seemed out of place with my then reality. But because I was adopted, I often felt different and alone. I did not have any friends who looked like me or who had been adopted.

When I entered my middle and high school years, I began to fantasize about my birth parents. I thought about how my mother gave birth to me when she was a teenager, and how ill equipped I would be to raise a child now that I had reached that age. I wondered if my birth parents thought about me, if they wanted to see me, if they regretted their decision. I thought about what their families might be like, and why nobody in their families took me in when I was a baby. I was curious if my father and his family even knew about my birth mother's pregnancy. I speculated about whether my birth parents had a relationship, or if it was a one night together circumstance, or something casual in between. I tried to imagine which parent was which race, and if that difference had entered into any decision making. I was curious if my birth parents' families knew each other, and if they did, if they were friendly.

I imagined that my birth parents shared my artistic temperament, and that they would understand me immediately in a way in which my adoptive family could never know me. When I had those thoughts, I felt disloyal, and tried to think of something else.

During college, I studied psychology and painting, and then I went on to get a master's degree in marriage and family counseling. I was attracted to that field because I thought about family issues incessantly, and did a lot of reading on the subject, even before I began to study it formally. On some level, it was part of my adoption journey. I painted as a serious hobby, and often the theme of my artwork was disjointed families."

I asked Sarah if she ever thought about trying to find her birth parents. She said:

"While I was studying, I began to think more and more about trying to find my birth parents. When I broached the topic with my parents and sister, they were negative about it. They said that the adoption was closed for a reason. They were concerned that I would be rejected by my birth parents and that it would be extraordinarily hurtful to me. They felt that I had a safe life and family, that my birth parents could turn out to be dishonorable people on a host of levels, and that I did not need to submit myself to such risk. They were also concerned, on some level, that they would lose me in that I would prefer my birth parents over them and their family. It was difficult for them to separate their needs and emotions from mine.

I understood their concerns, but there was something nagging inside of me that would not go away, and which they did not have to deal with for themselves. I pondered if my birth parents told the adoption agency the truth, and if there was some other story about their background that they did not disclose at the time of the adoption. If I had a medical illness, I became curious about what my medical history was. I longed to see if my birth parents looked like me, if I had some of their personality traits, if they had similar interests and talents to mine.

I became increasingly convinced that if I did not have more information about my birth parents, I could never resolve my own identity issues. It was hard enough to know who you are, without the added disability of not knowing where you came from, on a 'cellular' level. These were my issues, and my issues alone. My parents and sister could never understand, fully, as they knew where they came from. The families of both my adoptive parents were originally from the Netherlands, going back generations. They could trace their family tree with ease.

I continued to grapple with my adoption issues. I met my husband while I was in graduate school. He was a resident in anesthesiology at the time. His family was originally from Ethiopia. As an immigrant in this Country, he understood many of my identity issues and my feelings of being an outsider. As an African, he had an awareness of my racial issues as well. I discussed with him whether I should search for my birth parents. He was solidly behind it. He felt that I was strong enough to withstand any possible rejection from my birth parents, and, conversely, if I did not want to connect with them after I met them, I did not have to. He thought that I should search for them before they died or became incompetent, so that I would never have to experience a feeling of regret.

Once I became pregnant, I knew that I would have to start the search for my parents, and once I gave birth, I knew that I would need support in therapy to go through the process.

My husband remained supportive of the quest throughout, and for that, I remain grateful."

Over many months, we talked about her search for her birth parents, and her feelings around it. Over time, the story developed, as follows:

"My husband, as a doctor, thought that we should try DNA testing with a few companies, including Ancestry.com, 23andMe and FamilyTreeDNA. He reasoned that, at a minimum, we could obtain some medical information, which would be useful for me and for our child. He argued that it might also help in our search in a closed adoption situation. It took me some months to finally order the kits and to get started. I had many nightmares about it, and it made me feel anxious during the day. It took a bout of chickenpox, which our child contracted, to get me to do the testing.

It was a great relief that I was able to locate my birth mother through the DNA testing. I was not prepared. I thought that it would not be as simple as that, that we would have a long and tortured search, and that I would have to hire a private investigator because I did not have the time to do the search myself.

Then, as an added bonus, I found my mother's profile on Facebook. She had dark skin, and I had her hair and eyes. She was an art teacher at a local college, and a poet. Some of my lifelong questions had been answered from a single viewing on Facebook. She lived two hours away from me. I was able to locate her address and telephone number easily. First, I sent her a long letter telling her all about my life, and how I had been wanting to meet her for so many years and finally summoned the courage to search for her. I put my telephone number on the letter. I told her to look at my Facebook profile. I asked her to call me if she was willing to.

Two weeks passed and I had not heard from her. Although I was afraid of rejection, I decided to call her up. I heard her voice and identified myself. She told me that she been wanting to call me, but that she was afraid, and needed to summon up the courage, which she had not yet found. She cried on the telephone, and I did too. She said that she never forgot about me, and that she did not want to give me up for adoption but that she was a teenager when she became pregnant with me. She said that her family made her put me up for adoption for a host of reasons. She told me that there was much she wanted to tell me, but that she wanted to say it in person. I asked her when I could meet her.

My birth mother told me over the telephone that she was married to a much older man, and that he had three children by a prior marriage, but they never had a child together. She had developed endometriosis which prevented her from having another pregnancy. Her husband and her stepchildren did not know about me. Her parents were both deceased, and she had no siblings. Her aunts, uncles, and cousins who were still living did not know about me. She asked if we could meet at a diner on the highway, halfway between her home and mine. She was not yet certain if she would tell her husband, stepchildren, and other family about me, so she wanted our meeting to be in private. We arranged to meet a week later.

That waiting period was torturous. I knew from reading her Facebook profile, and from talking with her on the telephone, that she was as I had imagined her on many levels. She seemed artistic, sensitive, thoughtful, and caring. We clearly shared interests, and looked similar, although her skin was darker. She seemed to carry a great deal of shame about me and the adoption. I was worried about finding out more, but now that I had traveled that far emotionally, I knew that I had to complete the journey. We had not discussed my birth father at all, yet.

After that first telephone call with my birth mother, I told my adoptive parents and sister that I finally found her, and that I was going to meet her. We discussed it over a family dinner with my husband. They were visibly upset, and my husband had to run interference for me. They were concerned that I had opened a Pandora's box which could never be closed. They worried that my birth mother would be the kind of person who would take advantage of me and my generosity. They envisioned her as a drug addict, or someone on welfare. I explained to them that she was highly educated, had a good job, and a family of her own. I was not able to give them more details, as my birth mother had requested that I keep much of her life confidential until we had figured out what our relationship would be going forward.

All of the secrecy and shame was wearing on me. I had hoped, on a naive level, that my adoptive parents and birth mother would both be thrilled about my discovery, and that everyone would get together and I would be able to unite the two sides of me, finally. I knew, deep inside, that it was going to be more complex and difficult than that. I prayed that my situation would not be as bad as many other stories I had heard about adoptees reuniting with their birth families.

When I arrived at the diner on the appointed date and time, I immediately spotted my birth mother in a booth when I walked in. She stood up, we hugged briefly, and I immediately sat down across from her. We spoke for two hours."

I asked Sarah how it felt to meet her birth mother. She said:

"As always, I felt conflicting emotions. My overriding reaction was one of great relief. The mystery of my origins had finally been solved, and my birth mother would be able to provide me with many answers, which would be of great comfort to me, medically and otherwise. What I did not know at that time, however, was whether or not we would be able to develop a close and loving mother and daughter relationship going forward. My birth mother's initial hesitancy to reach out to me, and her not wanting to tell her family about me right away, were disappointing reactions from my perspective.

During our long conversation at that first meeting, I began to understand my birth mother's concerns better, and I knew on an intellectual level that they had nothing to do with me. She explained that when she was in high school in Chicago, even though the school was integrated, the black students stayed apart from the white students, and vice versa. She met my birth father, who was white, in an English class. They shared a love of poetry and creativity. They began to meet secretly, as her family and friends, and his family and friends, did not mix. It was a modern Romeo and Juliet story. Her family was African-American, and they were mostly teachers, and his family was from Ireland, and they were mostly police officers, firemen and union workers.

After a few months, they began having sex. One time they were using a condom, and it broke. That may have been when I was conceived. Her parents were religious Catholics, as were his. Nonetheless, they used birth control, although, obviously, it did not work. There was no way that abortion was an option for her, even if she had wanted it, which she did not. She broke up with him on the pretext that dating someone of a different race was too difficult for her, and her family had pressured her to break up with him. She told him that since they were both going to attend different colleges, it was a logical time for a break.

Her parents sent her away to relatives in a neighboring states when she started showing, she received home tutoring for school, and she gave birth there. After she delivered, I was taken away from her immediately and she never had the opportunity to hold me. She grieved for months on end. She said she wanted to keep me, but her parents forbade it, and they were not in a situation where they wanted to raise another child. A closed adoption had been arranged. She never told my birth father about the pregnancy, or the adoption. He went off to college, and so did she, as if the pregnancy and delivery had never happened.

I asked for more details about my birth father. She said that after she gave birth to me, she was never in contact with him again. She heard that after college he worked in law enforcement, and that he married a nurse, also from an Irish Catholic background, and that they had children.

We agreed that we would meet again, secretly, at the same location. In between the first and second meeting, I realized that even though I was getting to know my birth mother's story, and I had developed a great deal of empathy for her and her situation, it was not enough for me. I wanted to meet my birth father too.

At the second meeting, there were two problems which arose for me. One was my birth mother's reluctance to tell her husband and other family about me. This was going to be an impossible situation for me. I did not want to live in shame and fear of our relationship being found out. I wanted her to be proud of me, and to own up to what had happened so many years ago. I did not want to continue to meet her secretly. I told her that I would give her a year to get to know me, but if she could not tell her family about me after a year, I did not want to continue the relationship. We both cried. I understood her fears, but I told her that if her family loved her, they would be able to accept what happened to her so many years ago. She explained that it was not so easy. They would feel lied to and betrayed. They might not trust her after that. It might destroy all of their relationships. I, in turn, did not want to be responsible for ruining her family.

The second problem was perhaps even more complicated than the first. She refused to tell me the name of my birth father. The birth certificate listed the father as unknown, but from the details she gave to me, I knew that I could track him down with the help of an investigator. She told me that if I insisted on finding him, that she could not continue to have a relationship with me. I did not want to jeopardize my new relationship with her, but, on the other hand, her attitude about it was causing us a great deal of tension.

My feeling was that her attitude was selfish. I had a right to know my birth father, and to have the opportunity to see if he would accept me, and incorporate me into his family. He was one half of me. I understood that she was afraid that he would be angry with her for never telling him that he was a father. She was a shy person and could not face his potential hostility, but in truth, they did not ever have to discuss it or have contact. My relationship with my birth father was between me and him. They had not had any contact all of these years anyway. There would be nothing lost for her, and, potentially, everything to be gained for me.

I went home after that second visit with many more issues than I was prepared to deal with. If I insisted on my birth mother telling her family about me, and if I persisted in finding my birth father, my birth mother would abandon me again. If I let our relationship remain a secret, and if I stopped trying to connect with my birth father, I would always feel depressed, angry and unfulfilled. When I shared these dilemmas with my husband, he understand it all. He told me that I should discuss these issues with you, my therapist, and that he would support me no matter what I decided.

My adopted parents and sister, on the other hand, basically told me that they could have predicted that there would be problems, and perhaps I had made a mistake in looking back into the past. I knew that there was no way that they could comprehend what I was going through, so I forgave them, as I felt that their positions were from a loving place.

After much soul searching and angst, I decided to continue to meet my mother about once every two to three months, as our renewed relationship meant a lot to me. I was not willing to cut her off, and I hoped that she would eventually tell her family about me. I asked her to see a therapist about that issue, and she agreed to do that. Since I knew that she was working on the issue, even if it did not go the way I wanted it to, I could live with it. She has not yet agreed to meet my husband and child. I want my child to have another grandmother, but it may not happen. My birth mother's thoughts are that if she cannot tell her family about me, she cannot meet my family either. Her emotions are mixed and confused, and she is cutting herself off from so much joy. My heart goes out to her.

With respect to my birth father, I did not tell my birth mother, but I hired an investigator to find out some more details about him so that I could make a decision as to whether I wanted to contact him or not. Tragically, I learned that my birth father had been killed in the line of duty as a police officer approximately ten years ago. He was investigating a drug ring, and when he entered the apartment where the drugs were being sold, he was gunned down on the spot. When I confessed to my birth mother that I had investigated information about my birth father, and that he was no longer alive, we hugged one another and cried some more. I have not yet decided if I will ever contact my birth father's family."

Sarah continued in therapy for a few more years, and we spent a lot of time discussing her new relationship with her birth mother, what the parameters of that relationship will be, and whether she will contact anyone on her birth father's side of the family. Sarah wanted her child to be loved by as many family members as possible. Sarah wanted to expand the scope of her family for herself. When you are adopted, it is a situation for your entire lifetime. Not all family members want what the adoptee wants. She has been brave and loving throughout it all, and she is determined to come to terms with whatever develops in the future. Last I heard, she had adopted a biracial child.

Chapter Fourteen

Criminal Husband

"Rogue internet pharmacies continue to pose a serious threat to the health and safety of Americans. Simply put, a few unethical physicians and pharmacists have become drug suppliers to a nation."

Dianne Feinstein

An Italian American woman in her seventies named Angela came into treatment with me because of a serious dilemma. Her husband, John, a doctor, had completed his prison sentence and returned home. She was not certain if she should continue to live with him and remain as his wife. I asked Angela about her relationship with her husband. She told me:

"I met John in our old neighborhood on Staten Island when we were teenagers. He was four years older than I. Both of us had fathers in the construction business who were bosses in a major crime family of the Italian mafia. While it was not an arranged marriage, we grew up together, and fell in love.

John's father did not want him to be a mobster. He encouraged him to be a doctor, and paid his way through medical school. John always wore expensive clothes, drove luxury cars, went to expensive restaurants, and loved to gamble. He looked more like a gangster than a future doctor. He loved the fast life, and he dreamed of being extremely wealthy. He helped his father in the construction business during school vacations and in the summers to make money. He learned how to be tough and in charge. We both knew what our fathers did to make money, and we knew that they were criminals and murderers, although we never discussed it then. We wanted to have a large, close-knit Italian family.

We dated for many years, and then, while he was in medical school, we married. I had graduated from community college, but I had trouble with academics, as I had some learning disabilities, so I was grateful to be finished with formal schooling. Nonetheless, I did read a lot, and kept track of current events. I could keep up my end of a conversation. I had an artistic eye, so I could feather an attractive nest. I took speech lessons so that I could lose my Staten Island accent, and appear to be from an elite class. I had not prepared myself for any profession except that of wife and mother. I had street smarts, but I hid them from view. It was understood that I was not to compete with John on any level, and that he would be the chief in the teepee.

John expected me to look and act the part of the successful doctor's wife. He bought me expensive clothes, furs, jewelry and perfume, even before he was making money as a doctor. My father bought us a house in the neighborhood where our families both lived. I became pregnant right away, and had four children in ten years. My family encouraged me to be a good wife and mother. It was not expected that I would work as it was assumed that my husband would protect and provide for me, and that I would run the household. John hired help for me to take care of the house and the children. I went to the gym frequently, and made certain that I kept my figure, but I was largely confined to the home, and was mostly interested in my family. Our parents and other relatives were frequent visitors to our home. I had girlfriends in the neighborhood who shared a lifestyle similar to mine. We had lavish parties, and entertained frequently.

John was accustomed to being around people who had cash businesses and who liked to show off their money by living in huge homes with swimming pools and every other amenity. The grind of medical school, internship and residency wore on him. He became an anesthesiologist, and worked in a practice in Manhattan. He did that for about twenty-five years, but he became restless. Although he was making good money, it was not enough for him.

On my part, I became used to having whatever luxury goods I wanted. I had plastic surgery done all over my face and body. The more I had, the more John suggested I have. I hired people to handle every aspect of our lives. I lived like a queen, and I became addicted to having it all, and terribly afraid that it would all come tumbling down as I was completely dependent on my husband. After the children were grown, he discouraged me from working outside of the home, and I did not have confidence that I could succeed on my own in any event. I knew that he had girlfriends on the side, but I looked the other way. I did not want to give up the lifestyle I had. John began talking about starting a business so that he could earn even more money. I encouraged him to start a business, if that is what he wanted to do. He wanted fast money, and I did not discourage him from doing it. We were essentially partners in greed."

I asked Angela what happened to her husband's career, and how she felt about it. She told me what she had learned:

"John had a friend from medical school, Anthony, who had started a lucrative pill mill on Staten Island, New York. He wanted a partner, and John agreed to go into business with him. The mafia, historically, did not get involved with drugs, and John's father was against it. He so wanted his son to have a different life, to be a legitimate doctor, but John had absorbed what he learned from his father and friends all the years, and this was his way to quickly accumulate wealth. Money was his God. He ignored his father's warnings that he would become a drug dealer in a white coat.

John worked with pharmacists and medical assistants who were in on the deal. John and the others distributed millions of oxycodone pills, a painkiller, to drug addicts on the street. John and the other doctors wrote the scripts to patients they knew did not medically need the painkiller, who then sold them. They also wrote thousands of scripts for other controlled substances, such as buprenorphine and alprazolam, which is Xanax. They rarely examined patients, and some of the patients did not even visit their office. As the business progressed, they began to distribute drugs from internet sales as well.

Over the course of twelve years, John made millions of dollars in cash for writing thousands of prescriptions. The more money he made, the more he wanted to make. We never talked about how he made his money. I never visited him at work. We kept home and office separate. I later heard that pill-seeking patients would line up outside his office in the middle of the night, and that the neighbors were complaining and they started to call the police. I think that John must have paid off the police, because nobody came after him for many years. He kept moving to larger and larger offices to accommodate more and more 'patients'. He hired security staff to keep the addicts quiet while they waited to get into his office. I later learned that he regularly prescribed over one hundred oxycodone pills per patient per month, until he reduced all patients' monthly allotment when he became worried about scrutiny from law enforcement.

John started to have a split personality. He took some of the drugs during that time period. His behavior became more and more erratic, and I feared that he was becoming a drug addict himself. I told him that he had made enough money, and that he should quit before he ruined his health and our lives as a family. During the time that he was overindulging himself, he was extremely generous to everybody, including anybody in our families who needed money. He had become active in the community, and was considered a generous donor to many charitable causes. He was honored at many dinners of not-for-profit organizations. He was a pillar of the community, and a drug dealer, all rolled into one.

I could not confide in anyone because I did not want to be disloyal to John, nor did I want to get him in trouble. Everybody in the neighborhood seemed to know what he was doing, but looked the other way because he was such a generous neighbor. He was willing to help all with whatever they needed. Our children adored him, and so did all of our relatives and friends. Our household staff, and his office staff, respected and loved him.

It was as if I was living in a dream during those years. John bought properties all over the world, houses for each member of his family, luxury yachts, a private plane, original artwork, gold, silver, diamonds, and much, much more. He hid money in overseas accounts, and laundered money through legitimate businesses. I signed the tax returns, but I never knew the details of what he did until after he was indicted in federal court. Everybody was jealous of me because of our wealthy lifestyle. Nonetheless, I felt scared, alone, and vulnerable. I knew deep down in my soul that I was benefitting from ill-gotten gains. It weighed on me terribly. I kept losing weight, and everybody told me how great I looked because I wore a size 0 at my age.

The nightmare truly began one day when my doorbell rang. It was my neighbor, Rosa. She was in tears and hysterical. She shared with me the story of what had happened to her son. She had a son named Nick who was my eldest son's age. Nick and my son were in high school at the time, and had been friends since early childhood. Nick had been a star athlete who excelled at many sports, including football. During one football game, he was seriously injured, and broke his ankle. He went to a doctor, and was prescribed oxycodone for his pain. Nick was a gregarious, handsome, talented boy. He quickly became addicted to oxycodone, and spiraled downhill into becoming a junkie.

Rosa told me that Nick began stealing from her and other family members to get money for his drug addiction. He stopped attending school. He began to spend time with other drug addicts on the street in our community. He spent time in jail for stealing. She told me that Nick went with the other addicts to my husband's office on a regular basis, and were prescribed more drugs. Nick sold some of the drugs, and took some for himself. Nick never dealt directly with my husband, but he was aware that John was one of the principals of the practice. He told Rosa about it.

Nick was now on his fifth stint at a residential drug treatment center. Rosa said that she was afraid of what would happen to Nick when released. Rosa told me that they had exhausted all of their money, and they could not afford to send him to any more rehabilitation programs if he did not succeed in overcoming his habit that last time.

While she was telling me this story, we were sitting at my pool, which had a waterfall, in my backyard. My husband and I hired a landscape architect who had designed gardens all around the property. Household help provided us with elaborate drinks and food on polished silver. I was sporting a 10 carat diamond engagement ring. At that moment, looking into Rosa's face, and seeing her pain, watching her cry, and thinking about my own children, I truly realized what my husband's business was responsible for. Our luxuries were acquired off of the backs of young, innocent children, and other vulnerable people. I could not deny it any longer. We cried together, each in pain in our own ways. Her pain was far worse. What could be more heart wrenching than watching your child suffer? I told her I would try to help her in any way I could. I offered to give her money. She refused. I told her to keep in touch with me.

When my husband came home that night, I told him what Rosa had said. He became extremely agitated. He admitted to me that two of his office employees had fatally overdosed. I could see that he felt that his lifestyle was closing in on him. I begged him to get out of that business. I knew from his responses that he was in too deep.

About two months later, I called Rosa to find out how her son was doing. She cried and cried on the telephone. She told me that after Nick left the rehabilitation center, he started taking drugs again, and was arrested for breaking into a home in the neighborhood and stealing. After he was released from jail, and was out on bail, he died from an overdose. She told me that I should stop my husband from continuing to do his business. I cried with her. I tried to picture how I would feel if this happened to any of my children. I could not imagine how she could go on with her pain. I could not imagine how I could go on with mine. My son, who had been Nick's friend before he became a drug addict, knew of his death but did not share it with me because he felt guilty knowing that his father might in some way be responsible. His life was becoming poisoned with his father's misdeeds and my silence."

I asked Angela what she did at that point. She told me:

"I felt that I had to be loyal to my husband and to support him, even though I knew that what he was doing was wrong and was hurting so many people. I felt that it was my duty to try to keep the family together for the sake of our children. A few months later, my husband was arrested, and charged with illegally distributing millions of oxycodone pills, along with other crimes. His case was part of a larger federal drug bust. On some level, I was relieved. I did not want our children to have to deal with his actions any longer.

He pled guilty, and was sentenced to ten years in federal prison. I had to sell the house, and ended up living in a small apartment. My husband provided for me while he was in prison. There was money stashed away, and he made certain that I could pay all of my bills. I visited him regularly, and sometimes our children did too. I gained weight, and became obese. During the time that he was in prison, I asked relatives if they could give me money so that I could go for treatment to lose weight, and to get some plastic surgery. One of my relatives gave me money, and I never offered to pay it back. I felt desperate and needy. I was not thinking of other people's needs. When my relative told me that he had some business reversals, I still did not offer to pay it back. I am not certain why. I guess I was accustomed to people doing things for me."

I asked Angela if she thought about getting some training and looking for a job at that time. She told me:

"I felt too old, incapable and depressed. I stayed home a lot and slept. On the days that I felt better, I spent time with my children and grandchildren. I never worked outside the home for my entire life, and went straight from my parent's home to my husband's home. Frankly, it never occurred to me to look for a job.

Once my husband was released, he seemed like a changed man. At first he spent a lot of time with the family at home. He read a lot, and spent time alone in a home office I carved out for him in the apartment. He seemed embarrassed to face people outside the family. After a few months, he began to spend a lot of time on the telephone, and to have "business" meetings with people. He told me he was doing some consulting. I did not ask him what that meant. He continued to pay all of our bills.

He began to be restless. He felt that our apartment was too small and that he wanted to move into something larger. I did not ask him if we could afford it, or where the money would come from. The money always seemed to be there. He was more secretive than ever about financial matters. My position has always been that I don't need to know the money details as it will only upset me. That is what I learned growing up with my father and dealing with his mafia business, and that is what I carried with me, as my default reaction, into my marriage.

My husband asked me if I would sign my name to some legal papers so that the purchase of a home would be in my name since he could not use his name. I called one of my close relatives who was a lawyer. He told me not to sign anything. That is when I started to come to see you for therapy. I am not certain if I should leave my husband. I am concerned that he will continue to be in trouble, and will get me in trouble. On the other hand, as a senior citizen, I do not have many options.

My looks have faded and no other man will want me. People know that I am married to a former convict. The community is aware of what he did, and how he hurt other people. I am essentially a pariah, as is he. If I were to divorce him, I know that the money would miraculously dry up and he would say that there is no money for alimony.

In addition, our children and families think that we should remain together and would be extremely upset if we were to split at this point in life. They want me to sign the legal papers so that we can get a nice house to live in again. I want to be a good and loyal wife, mother, and grandmother. I was not raised to be a feminist. I do not know how to provide for myself. I do not want to provide for myself. I feel trapped, and know that it is too late to get out."

I asked Angela if she would be willing to live with one of her children. She said:

"My children do not want me to live with them. They want me to live with their father. They want us to have a house so that they can visit with their children. They think I am lucky that their father still wants to be with me, even though I am obese and depressed. They want me off of their hands, and they are happy that I have an alternative. Essentially, they don't want me to blow it. They will blame me for the divorce.

They love their father and think he is a good man despite what he has done. He makes them feel secure. He gives them money when they need it. He gives them love. They think that is enough. They don't see me as being as useful to them. Since I always had servants, I don't help them with their chores or cook for them. I can only minimally help with the grandchildren because of my physical disabilities. I do not have my own money to give them. They perceive me as a burden. They view their father as their savior. He presents himself as optimistic and a doer. They see me as a whiner and complainer. They think I am ineffectual. They are afraid that I will ask them for money."

Angela and I talked about her options over many sessions. She remained steadfast that she had no options. She eventually signed her name on the contract for the house. She moved into the house with her husband, and she told me that they are much happier there with all of the space. She was busy selecting furnishings for it, and upgrading the property with lavish plantings. She doesn't know how they have the money to pay for it, and, once again, she refuses to look closely at it. What she doesn't know will hurt her, but not yet, in any event. Her children and grandchildren visit them regularly there.

We talked about whether doing volunteer work, perhaps to help drug addicts, might help her to feel that she was making a contribution, and somehow balance out what her husband had done, and what she had ignored. It was my suggestion. She told me that such work would depress her. She prefers to walk around high-end malls, and to continue to get plastic surgery. She looks like she is wearing a death mask. I struggled to not judge her, but, given my values, which were quite different, it was a challenge. I cannot say that I enjoyed treating Angela. While she had many positive human qualities, her greed seemed to overshadow everything. I thought about all of the people in the news who made similar choices to those that she and her husband had made. It was difficult for me to feel sorry for her, and yet I did anyway. She seemed to be a victim of her parents' and husband's expectations of her, and then her children's. She could not summon the strength to be different.

The last time I spoke with Angela she had made peace with her decisions. She was enjoying her family. Her husband had not been re-arrested. She was surrounded by luxury again. For her, that would have to be enough.

Chapter Fifteen

On-Campus Sexual Assault

"Despite this inundation of rape imagery, where we are immersed in a rape culture—one that is overly permissive toward all manner of sexual violence—not enough victims of gang rape speak out about the toll the experience exacts. The right stories are not being told, or we're not writing enough about the topic of rape in the right ways. Perhaps we too casually use the term "rape culture" to address the very specific problems that rise from a culture mired in sexual violence. Should we, instead, focus on "rapist culture" because decades of addressing "rape culture" has accomplished so little?"

Roxanne Gay

Emily came to my office for the first time when she was in her late twenties. She wore simple, tailored clothing in muted colors. Her hair was light brown, and she wore little makeup and simple, understated jewelry. Her eyes were downcast, and her shoulders were slumped. She looked like someone who was trying hard not to be noticed; to blend in at best, or to disappear at worst.

She told me that it had taken her too long to seek help and that she should have been in my office for the first time after she was raped her freshman year in college. I asked her to tell me what happened. She spoke quietly, fighting back tears, and said:

"I grew up in a privileged family in a suburb of Chicago. My mother was a lawyer, and my father was a doctor. I had a younger brother whom I was close to and protective of. I attended liberal private schools, and was taught to be strong and that I could achieve whatever I put my mind to. In high school, I did not really date, but spent time in a large social circle. We would go to each other's homes on the weekends for parties. I did not do much drinking, and rarely experimented with drugs, although many of my friends did. I was quiet, bookish, and loved to read about and to make art. I knew that after college I wanted to work in a museum in some capacity, possibly as a curator.

I applied to and was accepted, early decision, to an arts college within a large university in the midwest. I was hoping to major in art history. Like many college freshman, in the first few months of college, I missed the security of my home and family. Instead of putting on weight, I started to lose it. My roommate, Grace, was extroverted, and had led a sheltered life in a small town in the midwest. She had a strict upbringing, became a bit wild, and wanted to experience what it was like to be free. College was her chance to break away from her background. I was happy to stay close to the dorm room and engage in quiet activities. She told me that I was being boring and that I needed to get out more.

Prior to Thanksgiving break, she prevailed upon me to attend a fraternity party with her one weekend. I had little interest, but wanted to please her, so I relented and said I would attend. Although it was not my style, she told me that I needed to 'up my game,' and wear makeup and a sexy outfit. She dressed me up in her clothes, and I felt pretty and excited about socializing. The top was tighter than I usually wore, and the skirt was shorter, but it was not outside the realm of what most college girls were wearing then. We bonded getting ready for the party.

We arrived at the fraternity house after the party was well underway. It was in an old Tudor style house on campus, near my dorm. The house was filled with people, the music was blasting, there were kegs of beer and other alcohol, and people were smoking joints and doing other drugs. Grace knew some students at the party, and she introduced me to them.

One of the fraternity boys, John, who was in his junior year, seemed to take an immediate interest in me. Grace knew John, and whispered in my ear that he was quite a catch. Apparently he was from an extremely wealthy family on the Main Line in Philadelphia. Old money. His secure future was assured. He was conservative looking, with short hair and preppy clothing. He was not my type, but handsome in a Tommy Hilfiger advertisement kind of way. I was flattered that he was so attentive toward me.

We talked a little bit, but the room was noisy, so it was hard to have much of a conversation. He shared with me that he was a business major, and planned to work in his family's company when he graduated. He offered to bring me a drink, and he insisted on my drinking it while he drank his. I had not eaten that much before the party, and I started feeling light headed. Grace went off with a boy she was dating, and I never saw her again that evening.

John asked me to dance, which we did, and then he brought me more drinks. He had his hands all over me and it was making me uncomfortable. In looking back, I suspect he spiked the drinks with something as my physical reaction was extreme. The room was spinning, and I could barely move. I was not used to drinking a lot, in any event. I told him that I was not feeling well, and that I needed to go home. I asked him to help me find Grace. He said that he had a room in the frat house, and that I could lie down for a few minutes there until I felt that I could walk home. He insisted that he could take care of me, and we could look for Grace later. He gently wiped my hair off of my face, and dabbed my forehead with a wet tissue. At that point I was feeling so ill, I had to believe him. I was incapable of resisting.

I do not remember much, but I know that I had trouble walking up the stairs and that he was practically carrying me. We went into his room, he brought me something more to drink, and I think I passed out on the bed. My entire body felt like a dead weight. I remember that I was immobilized, and was in and out of consciousness, but mostly unconscious. The next thing I remember is that my clothes were off, and John was on top of me with his penis inside. There were three other boys in the room. They were watching, and I think that at least one of them went on top of me after that too. There was blood all over the sheets as I was a virgin. I screamed and cried. John put his hand over my mouth. I heard the boys laughing about the fact that I was a virgin, and that this was a big score for them.

They must have carried me home, because the next thing I remember, I was in my dorm room, on my bed, dressed in the outfit I had worn to the party, with blood on my underpants. Grace never came home that night as she slept with the guy she was dating in his room. I was alone, and felt terrible shame. I could not remember exactly what happened, but I knew that I had been raped, probably gang raped, multiple times. I knew that I had not consented, and that I was incapable of consent."

I asked Emily if she told anyone about the rape, and if she reported it on a more formal basis. She said:

"I had this terrible feeling that somehow what had happened to me was my fault. I blamed myself for wearing suggestive clothing, which was out of character for me. I blamed myself for drinking too much, and for not being able to hold my liquor. It was a mistake to have trusted John and to have allowed him to take me to his room. I made it my mistake. I questioned whether I had given him the wrong signals. I was not used to a lot of male attention, and I was complimented that he chose me. I did want him to like me, but I did not want to have sex with him that night, and I did not want to be raped.

As I was lying on my dorm room bed, I thought about whether I should tell Grace. I decided that I did not want to tell her, because I knew that John was somewhat of a friend of hers, and she seemed to give him the seal of approval at the party. I did not want to tell my other friends, even old friends outside of college, because I feared that I would be stigmatized as the girl who had been gang raped. I did not want people to think of me that way. I was and always will be a shy introvert, and drawing attention to myself in that way was not something I could have tolerated.

I was inexperienced with boys and sex. I had been a virgin. I was not certain, on some level, if that is what happens at these parties, and if that was part of college life. I struggled with whether I should report it to the college and to the police. I determined that I did not want to report it. I made a decision, which was one of the worst decisions of my life, that I was going to bury what happened to me. I took a shower before Grace could get home. I washed out all of the blood from my clothing. I had watched enough Law and Order SVU television shows to know that I should have reported the rape, that I should not have showered, that I should have been examined immediately and submitted to a rape kit, and that I should have saved the clothing for DNA evidence without washing it.

When Grace came back to the dorm room, I pretended that nothing had happened, and told her that I got drunk, felt sick, and that I came back to the dorm. She asked me if I liked John, and I told her that he was not my type. She did not question me further, and I did not offer any other information.

After that incident I saw John in passing on campus. He smirked at me, and we walked right by each other. I looked down at his feet, and saw that he was wearing the same Gucci loafers he had on when I met him. Somehow, the sight of them, sickened me. They represented male privilege to me. I had this feeling of rage inside me, but I knew that I could not act on it. I thought I saw the other boys who were in the room that night in the dining hall. I thought that they were smirking at me too.

I went home for Thanksgiving after the incident. My parents could tell that something was wrong with me, but I did not confide in them about the incident. I felt ashamed, and I was afraid that they would blame me. I felt like damaged goods, but I did not want anyone else to know that I was damaged and to remind me of it. I told them that I was not happy at school, that it was too big and impersonal for me, and that I wanted to transfer to a smaller college closer to home. I knew that I could not face being on the same campus with those boys. I never returned to that college. I moved back home and took a semester off. I worked as a volunteer in a museum until I was accepted at a local college."

We talked about how she was not to blame for what happened to her. I suggested much reading on the topic, as she was a voracious reader and seemed to respond well to the written word. I asked her why she waited to go for therapy, and what had prompted her to see me at that point. She said:

"Ever since the incident happened, I kept thinking that I could put the rape behind me. I imagined that somehow, with the passage of time, I would be able to let go of it and that it would not impact me. But as the years passed, I realized that it was not going away. I thought about it every day. There were increasing layers of guilt. I punished myself thinking that, since I was not brave enough to report the rapes, other girls might have become victims of those boys, and that I could have helped to prevent that from happening.

While I was a freshman, we received pamphlets at orientation about sexual assaults, including rape. During my first semester, I remember hearing about another girl who had been raped before it happened to me. She had reported it to the college. I heard through the grapevine that the college authorities questioned her in such a way that they made her feel that she was to blame. The boy was a star athlete, and the school was intent on protecting him. She was brave enough to follow through with the police, but the prosecutor would not take the case because there was not enough evidence. She had taken a shower after the rape, and had waited too long to report it. After that, she was harassed by the rapist's athlete friends, and she eventually dropped out of school. The rapist suffered no consequences. Women's groups on campus had taken up her cause, to no avail.

I knew that there were many other incidents that I had not heard about, and that it was a common problem that often did not get reported. That was no comfort to me. When I thought about that story, I concluded that at least that girl tried to do something, even if it was not successful, which made her a better person than me. My negative feelings about myself took new forms in every aspect of my life. I constantly punished myself."

I asked Emily about the ways in which she punished herself. She said:

"After I graduated from college, at work, in the art museum, when I failed to stick up for myself, or was not brave enough to ask for an assignment, for help, for a raise, or for recognition, I tied my behaviors in to my belief that I was not worthy. I have been passed over for several promotions, and I am convinced it is because I project a lack of confidence and am perceived as too meek. My lack of self esteem is not restricted to the workplace.

My relationships with men have been severely impacted. I have trouble trusting men after what happened to me. I do not know if they are speaking truthfully to me. I have difficulties being sexually intimate with men. Sometimes when I am having sex, I get flashbacks of the rapes, and I start to cry. I have not told any of the men I dated about the rapes, but, obviously, they do pick up on something being wrong. I rarely relax and enjoy sex. My relationships last, at most, for three months. I am almost relieved when they end. The pressure of keeping up a relationship has been too much for me.

What is most disturbing to me is that my personality has changed since the rapes. I have become extremely anxious and fearful. I am afraid to take risks. I am afraid to travel. I do not go to parties. Obviously, I am not much fun. While I live in my own apartment now, I essentially go from home to work and back again. I take the same route to work, I eat the same foods every day, and I go to sleep at the same time. I only sleep about four hours a night, and toss and turn for hours. I have trouble eating, and have remained underweight since the incident. My cats keep me company. I am afraid to think of myself as a cat lady, but that is what I have become.

I do not have the confidence that I will ever be strong enough to marry and to have a family of my own. I worry about how I would protect my children from all of the bad people and things that might happen to them in the world. My parents have sensed that something is wrong, but we are not the kind of family who talk openly about our feelings. Nonetheless, they have urged me to see a therapist, because they think of me as someone who has failed to fully launch. They are both successful in their chosen professions. They do not see me as moving ahead in any sense. Their encouragement to seek help is what brought me to you."

Emily came to understand that she was suffering from PTSD, post traumatic stress disorder, and that she suffered from anxiety and major depression. We began a multicomponent treatment program which included pharmacological treatments. We spent a lot of time speaking about her thoughts and feelings, and explored ways that she could train herself to be more positive, and to have better coping skills.

I encouraged Emily to attend a support group for victims of rape, which she joined, reluctantly. Since she was shy, she was uncertain if she could share her feelings in so open a forum. She found that hearing other people's stories made her feel less lonely, and she became friendly with some of the women in the group. After a time, she decided to stop attending the support group, because she felt that she had gotten what she could out of it, and that hearing about other people's pain was no longer beneficial for her recovery. It started to depress her. She did maintain the friendships she had made, and saw those women outside of the group.

Emily came into my office for one session in an upbeat and elated mood. I asked her what was going on. She told me:

"I have been inspired by some of the women in my support group. I decided that speaking about my rapes to high school seniors and to college students might help me and them. I joined a speaker's bureau of an advocacy group, and they are training me. I determined that one way to expand myself, overcome my shyness, and assuage some of guilt is to educate other people and get outside of myself. The more I speak about the rapes, the easier it is for me to accept what has happened to me and to move on.

Part of my anxiety and depression stemmed from my feeling that I had no power, and that I had to conceal what happened to me. I cannot go back and accuse my rapists and seek justice now. Too much time has passed. But I can educate other students so that they understand the dangers on college campuses, and can avoid some of the pitfalls. And even if they should be unlucky enough to be in the wrong place at the wrong time, as I was, they will have tools to handle things from a place of strength. I did not have those tools."

I was gratified to hear of Emily's progress, and how she was helping to turn her life around through her own efforts. I asked her if she still thought about the rapes every day. She told me:

"I cannot pretend that the pain of the rapes will ever go away completely. I feel it in my body, soul and spirit. The intensity of the pain has faded somewhat, but will never disappear. I have accepted that. Something was taken from me the night those rapes happened. It was a trauma. It was a nightmare. Nobody deserves what happened to me. Through my therapy, I have learned not to blame myself. That makes living with what happened to me easier. I no longer feel guilty about how I handled the situation. I wish I had been stronger and reported the rapes when they happened, but I have forgiven myself for that, and feel that I am in some way making up for it by speaking and advocating for rape victims. I am no longer hiding in a room by myself. That is a lot of progress for someone as quiet and unassuming as me.

Part of my growth is now believing that I deserve to have a good relationship and to have a family. I have hope that I will meet a sensitive man. I will not talk about the rapes right away, but eventually I will open up about it as part of my history. Other women in my support group have gone on to have good relationships with men despite what happened to them. I look at them as role models. I now have told many of my close friends about the rapes. They have given me much support, and have told me that they wish they had known earlier so that they could have helped me.

I finally told my parents and brother what happened to me. We all cried. They felt badly that I did not confide in them sooner, but they said they understood. They are part of my cheering squad now. By letting family and other people in, I have expanded my circle of support, and I have to say, it feels much better."

Emily was an intelligent, sensitive woman. I had high hopes for her, but I knew that the road would not be easy. I have worked with other survivors of rape, and there are days of progress, and days of regression. I learned through Emily, who heard through her social grapevine and through social media, that the boys who raped her, and who watched her being raped, are all successful businessmen, with families and children. I wondered if they ever thought about what they did. I wondered if they ever felt badly about it. I wondered if they rationalized it by blaming Emily for it. I wondered if they remembered it, or if they were too drunk at the time. I wondered how they treated their wives, daughters, and female co-workers. I wondered how they continued to displace all of their rage.

Afterword

As I created these stories, it became more and more apparent to me that even with the best efforts of a caring therapist, as represented by Esther Mahler, who had a profound understanding about the societal context in which these patients existed, there were certain situations that therapy alone cannot fully improve.

Coping skills may not be enough, for example, for a mother who rightfully fears that her ex-husband may kidnap their child again, and for a teen whose nude pictures have been placed on the internet by a vengeful ex-boyfriend and will remain somewhere on the web forever. For those types of issues, even the strongest laws, and their strict enforcement, may not fully remedy the situation either. Sometimes a therapist cannot prevent, or cure, a lifetime of pain.

There are many terrible ways in which people treat one another, and themselves. Women and children have oftentimes been targets, historically. Women need to understand what they can control, and what they cannot, and how to best exercise their wisest powers. Surely therapists help with that. So can the enforcement of just laws.

Sometimes the crises result from family background, from personal chemistry, from the historical period in which women live, or from a combination of these components.

These components can result in certain bad choices being made by women in crises. Therapists can assist with that.

I would not discount luck as a hidden component either. The most difficult crises can be those caused by another human being, such as a rapist, which a woman cannot always prevent or control. The randomness of that experience is surely what makes therapy a tremendous challenge. The Esther Mahlers of the world will always have their place. What they can achieve is a continued discussion.

Acknowledgements

I am grateful to Dr. Amos Grunebaum and Rae Ellen Vitiello for reading the draft of the book and for providing helpful edits. I appreciate my time spent as a lawyer on family and criminal court cases, which helped me to understand the issues facing women in multiple forms of crises, and allowed me the opportunity to work with many therapists. I am thankful for my continued time spent working with women lawyers on bar association committees to try to improve the lives of women, children and families.

Most of all, I am appreciative of my daughters, Katie and Eve, for always supporting my time working on these issues as they were growing up, and for becoming strong, self-reliant, productive, caring women and family members.

About the Author

Susan L. Pollet lives in New York City, and has been an attorney for over forty years, primarily in the area of family law. She has published over sixty articles on varied legal topics, including family and criminal law. She was President of the Westchester Women's Bar Association, Vice President of the Women's Bar Association of the State of New York, Executive Director of Pace Women's Justice Center, Director of the New York State Parent Education and Awareness Program, and a prosecutor. She has a strong desire to provide the public with information about interesting people who give us hope.

She is also a published author and artist. In 2019, her first novel was published by Adelaide entitled "Lessons in Survival: All About Amos." She created the collage for the book cover, and also painted the portrait which appears on the cover of her second novel, "Through Walter's Lens," also published by Adelaide, in 2020. Two of her short stories were published by Adelaide in 2019 and 2020 in their literary award anthologies. Susan painted the portraits and created the collage for this book cover.

ngramcontent.com/pod-product-compliance
ng Source LLC
rsburg PA
20019030726
B00007B/2176